LOVE'S UNCERTAIN TOMORROWS

Suddenly, Greg Cameron bent and kissed her. She was too surprised to resist, and soon aware that his lips were firm and good against hers. He was not gentle, and yet not rough, either. It was a surprising sensation, which touched her senses and sent them into erratic patterns.

Brooke Summers, San Francisco's first tv anchorwoman, had always held tight rein on her emotions and her future. But somehow things seemed to be slipping from her. . . .

LOVE'S FAR HORIZON

Lee Roddy

David C. Cook Publishing Co.

ELGIN, ILLINOIS—WESTON, ONTARIO

Published by David C. Cook Publishing Co.

ISBN 0-89191-540-0
LC 81-69258

To Grace and Cleland Noret

Chapter One

Brooke Summers barely paused at the stop sign, then careened right a half block, ignoring the angry horn blast of a taxi parked in the narrow street. Brooke hardly slowed as she turned right again, out of the city's high August fog, and zoomed down a ramp into an underground parking lot with the sign: KBRG Private Parking.

Her tires squealed as she whipped into a parking space opposite the garage elevator. But she cut too sharply past a low-slung foreign sports car, which was parked next to her. The red Italian car suddenly seemed to leap like a living creature. During the next fraction of a second, Brooke heard the sound of crunching metal and breaking glass.

"Oh, no!" she moaned. Quickly, she glanced around to see if anyone had witnessed the "fender bender." Except for a man at the elevator behind her, she saw no one.

But when the man yelled, "Hey!" she knew she was caught. She glanced into the rearview mirror to get a better look at the man who hurried toward her. He was about six-two, trim, with dark, curly hair, which spilled over his right eye. But the eye was dark, black—filled with anger.

Brooke took only a second to remember what her father, the politician, always said. "The best defense is a good offense." She swung her long, slender legs out of her car, and quickly adjusted the fawn-colored, floppy brimmed hat she knew looked well on her. Then she spoke sharply.

"What's the idea of parking your car in my space?"

The tall, slender man made a choking sound as he took the last few purposeful steps to survey his crumpled left rear fender.

"You crazy?" he demanded, waving one arm at the fender and the other at her. "You're the one who hit my Fiat. And I'm parked legally, well inside the white lines. See?"

Good! He's defending himself, Brooke thought as she flashed her wide smile. At age twenty-five, she was nearly five-seven, almost too narrow at the waist, but nicely proportioned everywhere else. She let her hazel eyes sparkle in a way she'd learned was disarming.

"Look," she said, keeping the smile laced in place. "I'm going to let you off easy because I'm due upstairs in front of the cameras shortly. I don't have time to argue." She turned toward the elevator.

The reference to television usually awed

people. Brooke had long ago learned how to use her celebrity status as the only anchorwoman in the West (all other stations required that a man co-anchor the evening news) to her advantage.

But the tall man wasn't buying her diversionary tactics. Brooke had only taken two steps toward the elevator when he strode beyond her and then spun around to face her. "Not so fast. Let's see your driver's license!"

"What? Really, Mr. . . . Mr. . . ."

"Cameron. And you're . . . ?"

"Brooke Summers . . . of Channel Three." She hesitated just a moment, and then turned desperately toward the elevators. "Look, I'm terribly late! Next time, don't park improperly!"

"Wait a minute, Miss Summers! You're not going to pull that stuff on me!"

His last words were muffled by the horn of a late model sedan, which pulled up beside the couple. "Oh, Scotty! Will you talk to this gentleman about his car? I'm late for my show!"

Before Scott Barr had disengaged himself from the front seat Brooke slipped through the doors of the elevator as it discharged passengers. She punched the button and the doors closed, shutting out the defiant evenly tanned man, dressed in tight black pants and a gray silk sports shirt that was open at the collar.

Scotty will take care of that guy. What was his name, anyway? Brooke wondered as the elevator sped upward. Scotty was one of the most stable, level-headed people Brooke knew. Someone she could rely on. And his dark blond hair and handsome smile made him a fun escort.

But Brooke didn't have time for idle musing.

She forced her mind to think about the "Six O'Clock News," which she'd do in three and a-half hours.

She barely spoke to the security guard as she was admitted to the KBRG offices. But the voice of Hal Humphries, the news director, broke into her mental listing of the things that had to be done before she went on camera that evening.

Humphries believed in direct action, so he sometimes skipped his underling, the assistant news director, to speak directly to on-camera personalities. "What's the matter with you lately, Brooke?" he demanded. "I don't like the way you handled yourself last night."

Some of the news crew had caught the tone of his voice and looked up to observe the confrontation.

"Could we discuss this in your office?" Brooke said.

Humphries led the way into his plush carpeted office and closed the door. He sat in the overstuffed chair behind his glass-topped desk and frowned at Brooke. His heavy dark brows slid down over pale blue eyes, which always seemed purposely cold to Brooke. The right forefinger that he waved at Brooke showed yellow nicotine stains.

"Last night, on the 'Eleven O'Clock News Report,' you snickered when you did that reader on the local guy who was arrested for selling stock in a solar-powered vacuum cleaner. Keep your face straight, Brooke!"

"That was the same joker who was selling a solar-powered machine to turn leaves into gold," Brooke protested. "The bunko squad nabbed him for that a year ago. I can't believe people are stupid enough to fall for such ridiculous cons. Besides, the writers threw that story in to lighten up the show."

"No editorial opinions, Brooke, including smirks that suggest what you're thinking!" Humphries paused, then demanded, "Don't you like doing the anchorwoman bit anymore?"

It was his favorite ploy. Humphries hadn't wanted to have a solo anchorwoman. He had spent twenty years in the newsroom, idolizing Walter Cronkite and the other greats. A man was best suited for the lead position, Humphries maintained, or at least, a co-anchorman. But the "Old Man," who owned KBRG in San Francisco and six other stations in major markets throughout the country, had demanded an on-camera, female personality, around whom the entire news team revolved. He had also suggested the ideal person: Brooke Summers, a feature reporter and news co-anchor at the ABC network affiliate in downstate Bakersfield.

Brooke knew her good looks and her dad's friendship with the "Old Man" had gotten her this chance, even though she had drawn top ratings in the smaller Bakersfield market. But she was determined to live up to the "Old Man's" recommendation by proving her competence as a media professional day in and day out. Humphries seemed equally determined to prove her inadequate and have her replaced. The last year had been a series of skirmishes to see who would win.

Brooke knew she hadn't responded to the news director's question. Her first inclination had been to yield to the internal voice of doubt, which sometimes said, *Maybe Humphries is*

right? Maybe I'm just not that outstanding.
Brooke knew the first local anchorwoman had
to be just that much better than any of the an-
chormen. But then her thoughts turned to her
father's praise of the admiral under whom he'd
served in World War II. "Attack! Attack! Attack!" Bull Halsey had always said.

"Look," Brooke began, leaning toward the
squat tv executive, "you know that since I've
been on the evening news, your ratings have
jumped from 29 to 40 percent of the audience. In
a four-station market, that's big business!"

"Not lately!" Hal responded with a slight
smirk as he slowly stood up. "In the last rating
period, Channel Ten was ahead of us. With a
new period coming up, you'd better think of
something to hype your news segment."

He stopped but Brooke got the implied threat.
She had already been renegotiating her contract, which would expire next month. KBRG's
number one sports announcer, Bart Conner,
and weatherman, Jerry Hansen, had received
good contracts, with substantial advances. But
because of the news director's bias against
Brooke, the contract offered her had been un-
satisfactory; they were still haggling over several important details.

Brooke had been a sensation when she had
become the first solo anchorwoman in the Bay
area the previous year. But just before the last
rating period, the co-anchorwoman on the most
competitive station had begun wearing daring
outfits on camera. Brooke knew Humphries
wouldn't admit that the predominantly male
audience at six o'clock had responded to the
other woman's enticement.

"Why me?" Brooke continued. "Why're you talking to me about ratings when Bart and Jerry are in front of those cameras each night, too?"

Instead of responding, and taking the defensive, Humphries threw an ultimatum back at Brooke. "Come up with some hot feature for both the 'Six O'Clock' and 'Eleven O'Clock News Report.' And don't waste any time. The next ratings are only a month away. . . . Now you'd better get with the assignment editor. And don't be late for the production meeting!"

Brooke left the news director's office and went mechanically about her regular afternoon duties. By three o'clock, she'd learned there were no breaking stories and no news conferences, so she was calm when she entered her own office and the production meeting began. It was a misnomer, for it was actually a news meeting.

Brooke didn't mind the vanity that always flavored these meetings. The assistant news director, the six o'clock news producer, the eleven o'clock producer, and the news writer—all of whom were men—liked to believe that they were solely responsible for the station's success. Each man was extremely competitive, and she knew that the atmosphere kept her on her toes. But she was glad the meeting was in her office, which was home territory, and made her feel more relaxed.

"What've we got?" the assistant news director asked to open the short meeting. George Harper was a rumpled man in his late twenties, wearing an open shirt, loafers, and wire-rimmed glasses.

Brooke hardly listened as they ran down the list: a triple murder, a feature on third graders writing the president, some aged residents being evicted in a condo conversion, some navy ships entering the harbor, and a hassle in city hall over the firing of some minor official.

Brooke's eyes reviewed her wall of plaques and trophies which reminded her that she was doing well in a predominantly man's world—despite what Hal Humphries said. "First prize, spot news for excellence in covering the Logan Hotel fire"; "Byline Award from the San Francisco Press Club"; "Best Newscaster Award"; "The Deadline Club"; and several others.

By the end of the meeting Brooke felt better about things. She knew she could even tolerate the union makeup man, who made a great show of laying out his products when Brooke was sure she could use a simple damp sponge to apply Tan Number Two to the tip of her nose and chin as she had in Bakersfield.

Scott Barr was waiting for Brooke when she went downstairs for dinner after the "Six O'Clock News Report." She knew he'd come to the station to discuss some kind of deal with management. But he wouldn't tell her about it until he had some firm commitment from the station's execs.

"I've been waiting to hear what happened," Brooke admitted after Scotty had greeted her.

"Still can't tell you about my confab with the big boys," he teased, his eyes reflecting his good humor. "But I can tell you about the guy with the crumpled fender."

"Well?" Brooke said as they started toward the coffee shop.

"His name is Gregory Cameron, and he was a

little steamed when you ran off like that. I tried to smooth his feelings, but I'm not sure you've heard the last of him."

Brooke put her arm around Scotty's broad shoulders to thank him for rescuing her. She could always count on Scotty. They'd met soon after she'd joined KBRG on one of her first assignments. Scotty, a private pilot, had flown the news crew up the coast to do a story on a beached whale.

Brooke frowned. "Cameron? Where've I heard that name before?"

"I don't know, Brooke. He's obviously well-off, judging from the way he dresses, and especially that car you kissed with your bumper.... By the way, his car was properly parked."

She stopped and looked into Scotty's concerned eyes. "You're saying it was my fault?"

"From what Dr. Cameron said, he's going to let a judge decide."

"Doctor? . . . Now I know where I've seen that name. He's always in the society pages and once . . ." Brooke let her voice trail off.

Scotty finished for her. "Once he appeared on Channel Ten with Patty Burton."

Brooke entered the coffee shop and ruefully shook her short, brunette hair. "She beat me to a good story, Scotty."

Scotty held up two fingers to the hostess who motioned for them to follow. "I must say, Brooke, you're not taking this whole thing well."

"Just what do you mean, Scotty."

He seated her and sat down across the table before answering. "Nobody ever accused Senator Jak Winter's daughter of ducking out on a difficult scrap. But . . ."

"Please, Scotty! Not so loud." Brooke glanced around the restaurant. Some diners were sneaking thoughtful glances at her. She was used to it now: they always thought they knew her, or had seen her somewhere. It would take them awhile to figure out who she was. "You know I don't want to have dad's name mentioned in connection with mine."

Scotty chuckled. "Still going to make it on your own, huh, Brooke? Your own name and all the rest?"

She let the remark pass. Her mother had been a pioneer television celebrity. Her father had been reelected six times and now served as the California Senate majority leader. The successes had had an adverse effect on Brooke's only brother. But she was born fighting, as her father used to say. She'd taken a different last name when she graduated from college. She wanted people to know her as Brooke Summers, successful tv newscaster, not the daughter of the big politician up in Sacramento. Few people in the Bay area knew she was related to her famous parents.

"I like my life as it is, Scotty. I'm going to keep it that way."

He put down his menu and looked steadily across the table at her. "For how long, Brooke?"

She managed a smile, although this wasn't her favorite topic. "For a while. Someday I'll find the right man, and then we'll see."

Brooke saw Scotty's fair skin redden slightly. He involuntarily brushed a tanned hand across his dark blond hair, which tended to curl ever so slightly. Instantly, Brooke realized he considered himself that man. She reached long, slender fingers across the table and touched his hand. "Scotty, let's not talk about me. Tell me what else the man said."

"Doctor Cameron? Oh, something about going to file hit-and-run charges against you."

"He wouldn't!"

Scotty raised a pale blond eyebrow above strong blue eyes that glinted with a sudden interest. "Oh, I'm not so sure about that! Of course, nobody was injured, but you did leave without even giving him your driver's license. And he did ask for it."

Brooke turned to the menu. She felt anger rising inside her. As if it wasn't enough that she needed something to hype her television appearances. Now some society doctor with a quick temper was threatening her. And over such a trivial thing.

"Brooke," Scotty said softly. "I sure wish you'd quit barging through life with your eyes on only one goal."

Before she could reply, a giggly teenager with scraggly blonde hair towed a reluctant, pimple-faced young man to the table. "You're Brooke Summers, aren't you? I've seen you on television! Would you give me your autograph?"

Brooke ordinarily enjoyed the attention, but tonight she wasn't in the mood for demanding fans.

"I don't have anything to write on," she protested. "And nothing to write with."

The teenage girl snatched the menu from Brooke's hand. "Here! Sign this! Use my pen!"

Brooke forced a professional smile and obeyed. As she was finishing her quick signature she heard the girl say to Scotty, "Are you somebody?"

Brooke tried to break into the offending girl's words, but it was too late. Still, Scotty didn't seem to care.

"I have the honor to be a friend of the famous Brooke Summers. That's enough for me."

The teenager turned questioningly to her reluctant male companion and then back to Brooke, retrieving her pen. "Oh, thanks, Brooke!" She turned triumphantly away, towing her friend behind her with a firm hand.

"I'm sorry, Scotty," Brooke said softly.

"It's OK, Brooke."

She studied his face. He was slightly pink with inner emotions, but his eyes were calm. "You really meant that, didn't you, Scotty?"

"I'll always mean it," he said evenly.

Brooke looked steadily into Scott's blue eyes and knew he was in love with her. He'd never said a word, but Brooke was sure. She turned to a nearby table and retrieved another menu, focusing her eyes on the print. The sudden image of the angry doctor crowded into her mind, easing out the look she'd just seen in Scott Barr's eyes.

Scotty was saying something. Brooke blinked, then apologized.

"I'm sorry, Scotty; what were you saying?"

A flicker of shadow crossed his eyes. "It's OK, Brooke," he said evenly. "Nothing important."

"Please, Scotty! I didn't mean to be rude, but my mind was on that man's threats. Please!" She reached long fingers across and barely touched his fingers on the menu. "What were you saying?"

He studied her thoughtfully, his lips puckering slightly in thought. Then a grin touched his mouth and danced in his eyes. "I said," he replied with a broadening smile, "I have a surprise for you."

"Oh, what?"

Scotty shook his head. "Since you weren't interested a moment ago, I don't think I'll tell you."

She realized he was teasing her. "Oh, come on, Scotty! I'm dying to know."

He lowered his eyes to the menu again. "No. You missed your chance! You'll just have to wait."

Brooke wasn't going to wheedle. But all through the meal her curiosity battled with images of Dr. Cameron. Could he really make trouble for her? And what was Scotty's surprise?

Chapter Two

The doorbell rang insistently. Brooke heard it from deep in restless sleep. Finally, she realized what it was and switched on the nightstand lamp.

"3:15," she moaned, brushing her hair from her eyes to take another look. "Who in the world—?"

She swept a long green robe down over her shoulders and fumbled with the zipper. The doorbell was being punched repeatedly, either angrily or urgently. Brooke slid her feet into open-toed slippers and hurried out of the one bedroom in her apartment and across the living room.

She peered through the tiny peephole and angrily shook her head. Then she loosened the night chain, slid back the dead bolt, and opened the door.

"Erik! What on earth's the matter?"

Her brother stumbled into the room and flopped heavily in a modern, chrome-trimmed chair. He was taller than Brooke, overweight at twenty-three, and had a shallow complexion, which suggested his life-style.

Brooke's alarm subsided into anger as she turned from the door and scrutinized Erik Winter with hot hazel eyes. "What is it this time?" she demanded, hands on hips, "drugs or booze?"

"Neither!" Her brother made a defensive motion with a rather limp right arm. "I'm just tired and don't feel like driving home!"

"You're in no condition to drive anywhere, let alone to mom and dad's. I'll fix you some coffee; then I want an explanation!"

Some time later her brother sat hunched on the kitchen barstool, his head bobbing over his fourth cup of black coffee. The cup was nearly empty, but Brooke didn't try to refill it. She estimated her brother was alert enough to respond to her questions.

She seated herself on the adjacent stool and studied him through half-closed eyes. "How do you feel?" she asked quietly. Her anger had given way to concern. Although he was only two years younger, Erik still lived off his parents through the pretense of attending college.

The senator's children had been assured of parental support as long as they remained in school. Brooke had taken full advantage of her parents' backing and had graduated cum laude from Stanford University with a degree in communications. She had appreciated her "free ride" but had felt a lot better when her

Bakersfield job had given her financial independence. Erik, on the other hand, had been to four different Bay area universities. He had failed out so many times, and changed his major so often, no one knew if he would ever finish his B.A.

"I'm OK, sis," Erik finally replied.

"You haven't called me 'sis' in a long time, Erik." Brooke knew he was appealing to the close relationship they had felt as children. For years she had defended his behavior and refused to admit his weaknesses. Now that he was purposely making a mess of his life, she felt partly responsible. They had *all* spoiled him.

Erik raised his eyes. They were bloodshot, but the pupils didn't seem dilated. Brooke had learned to make such quick appraisals. She dreaded what the media would do if the long-term senator's son had his picture splashed across the papers for some illegal activity.

"I think I'm ready to rest," Erik said. "OK if I crash on your couch again?"

"Of course."

Erik's feet stuck over the edge of the sofa as he squirmed to find a comfortable position. He was sobering, and his demeanor had turned antagonistic by the time Brooke could get an extra quilt out of the closet.

Brooke saw it coming. There was nothing she could do except turn off the lights and try to get to bed before he began his usual harangue. "Good night, Erik."

"What's your hurry, Brooke?"

"It's late. I've got to work tomorrow, and you need some sleep. See you in the morning."

His voice followed her into the bedroom. "Got

to be all bright-eyed for the big red eye of the tv camera, huh, Brooke?"

She ignored the taunt.

He was silent a moment, and Brooke started to sigh with relief as she slid into bed.

But her brother's voice came through the darkened room to her. "Still using that phony television name, huh?

"Good ol' Brooke!" His voice was stronger. The coffee had obviously cleared his head. "Going to make it all by herself in this big ol' world! Yeah! That's my big sister, all right. But where's it get you? Drove off every guy who ever looked at you, being so independent."

Brooke's reply slipped out before she could stop herself. "You've never liked any man I dated, and you know that! By the time they pass your inspection, they're discouraged."

Erik chuckled in the darkness. "Proves my point. You need someone who's not scared off so easily. Like that Scott guy. What's his name?"

Brooke listened in silence. Did that indicate her brother favored Scotty a little? Or was that just a way to get her to engage in conversation? She decided not to answer.

"You seen anybody else you like better?" her brother called through the darkened apartment.

Instantly, the image of the dark, brooding Dr. Cameron formed in Brooke's mind. She tried to push the thought away, but it stayed. She remembered the open-throated silk shirt and the tanned face with the straight nose and dominant cheekbones.

"No," she called softly. "Nobody else."

There was silence. Brooke hoped her brother

was going to drop the subject, but he spoke again. "You mad at me, sis?"

Brooke couldn't suppress a feeling of compassion. "No, Erik. I'm not mad."

"You got troubles?" he called.

She hesitated. "Nothing I can't handle."

It was a mistake. He picked up on it. "Want to talk about it?"

"No. And good night."

She heard her brother padding across the living room floor. He loomed in the open bedroom door, the blanket over his shoulders. "What kinda troubles, sis?"

Brooke sighed. "Nothing much. I clipped some guy's fender with my car, and he's threatening to sue me or something."

Erik chuckled. "Wish I didn't have any worse troubles than that."

Brooke wanted to ask what his problems were, but she'd often tried that without results. Whatever her brother was doing besides drinking and using drugs was a secret he managed to keep even when his guard was down.

Erik spoke again. "You got any worse problems?"

"Well, if you must know, the news director isn't happy with me right now. With contract renewal time coming up, I'm going to have to come up with some gimmick to hype my spot, or I'm in trouble."

Erik was silent. Finally he spoke. "Now that's real trouble, Brooke. What happens if you fail? Going to give up the career and get married like a normal girl?"

"Good night Erik!" Her anger sounded clearly in the darkened apartment.

Erik took one last look in her direction, then turned away from the door. "Yeah. My big sister's got real troubles. Now maybe you'll know how it feels." She heard him settle onto the couch. In a moment, he was snoring.

Brooke woke the next morning with a headache, which throbbed even more when she remembered Erik was in the next room. Of course, he was still asleep. Was he in real trouble this time? she wondered as she dressed for work.

She was just leaving the apartment without breakfast when the phone rang. Since she was standing near it, she swooped it up before the first ring had been completed. "Hello?" she said softly.

"Brooke?" She recognized Scotty's voice in her ear. "That you?"

"Yes."

"Why're you whispering? Everything OK?"

"My brother's asleep on the couch."

"Again? . . . Sorry! None of my business!"

"It's OK, Scotty. Why're you calling so early?"

"You know that surprise I told you about? . . . Would you like to know what it is?"

"Of course. Why do you think I keep asking you?"

"Then stop at the airport on your way to work today."

"Scotty, you know the airport's far away from the studio."

His voice was urgent. "It'd please me if you'd stop by the airport, Brooke."

She hesitated. "Well, if it's important, Scotty, of course."

Brooke eased the receiver back into the cradle and moved quietly out the door.

Even though she would be late for work she took the freeway south toward the peninsula following the airport signs until she came to the road that led to Executive Airport. She swung her car onto the frontage road and drove up to the first row of hangars.

Scotty was standing by the first open hangar. Brooke waved and he was beside the car when she parked. Quickly he took her hand and led her around the back side of the long row of metal hangars. He stopped just beyond the corner and swept out his right hand dramatically.

"Feast your eyes on that!"

Brooke blinked. "A helicopter, Scotty?"

"Not just a helicopter, Brooke!" His voice was vibrant with excitement. "That's a very special chopper! Can land on water if necessary. Just pull the lever on that bottle of nitrogen overhead and arm the floats. They'll expand in seconds. . . . Flies one hundred and forty to one hundred and fifty knots. With a full house, two people sit next to the pilot and the other two passengers in the backseat. But normally, we'll be carrying only one passenger."

"We?" Brooke asked.

"KBRG and me. Brooke, they not only bought this news helicopter, but they hired me as their pilot! How about that?"

Brooke felt a certain letdown. And alarm. If the company had put that much money into a newscopter to bolster their sagging ratings, it indicated they might trim costs somewhere else. Like the news team.

Scotty sensed her disappointment and took

his eyes off the new chopper. "Hey! What's wrong, Brooke?"

"Nothing, Scotty! Nothing at all!" She tried to force a smile. "It's a beautiful aircraft, and I'm delighted you're going to be flying it."

"But—?" he prompted.

Brooke started to shake her head, but Scotty's strong hands were on her shoulders. He forced her to look up into his eyes. "What's the matter, Brooke?" he asked softly.

She shook her head and gently freed herself from his grip. "I'm happy for you, Scotty; really, I am. But I've got a lot on my mind.... I'm sorry."

She turned away and he followed her around the hangar and back toward her car. "Your brother?"

"Partly."

"Partly?"

She nodded as he swung into step beside her. "I suspect that whirlybird means KBRG is going to cut expenses somewhere else."

"Like you?"

"Like me."

"Hey! No problem! Just tell me what you want. I'll see what can be done about it."

His seriousness made Brooke smile. "What can you do? I mean, Scotty, it's going to take a miracle for me to come up with an idea that will hype my ratings and get me a renewed contract. Humphries wants me out; he's just waiting for a good excuse."

"If anyone lacks wisdom . . ." Scotty began.

"I know!" Brooke stopped him with a hand on his forearm. Scotty had quoted the verse to her before. She knew the gist of it. "God gives liberally to those who ask," she repeated to him. "But remember, Scotty, I stopped asking a long time ago." Scotty's references to his Christian beliefs made Brooke feel uncomfortable and even a little guilty, so she ended the conversation abruptly. "Congratulations on your new job and the helicopter.... Now I've got to get to work. I'm already late."

They walked back to her car in awkward silence. He opened the door for her and closed it when she was seated. She waved, managed a brief smile, and drove off, feeling a tightening in her throat that she couldn't explain.

Her tension got worse when she arrived at the studio. She found herself on a collision course with Hal Humphries as she walked down the hall to her office.

"Brooke, you're just the one I was looking for! How you doing on a good idea for your segment of the news?"

Rather than admitting she hadn't thought of a thing, she tried to bluff. "I've got a couple hot ideas," she said, stalling for time.

"Such as?" The heavy, dark eyebrows puckered over those baleful blue eyes.

"Oh," Brooke said, "there's a possible series on new careers for women. . . ."

Hal broke in with an impatient wave. "I'm tired of all this women's lib stuff."

Brooke hesitated, then said, "Hal, some of my best ideas are still in the formulation stage."

"Well, the next time we meet, don't waste my time with lightweights. Lay the big idea on me. Understand?"

Brooke nodded, but the ND was already heaving his bulk down the hallway. Brooke had struck out. She didn't dare do it again.

Chapter Three

It was well after midnight when Brooke had unwound enough to drive home. She was surprised to see her brother sitting on the step outside her apartment. Ordinarily, after he'd come in as he had the previous night, he would take off and not return for some weeks. Brooke sensed that this visit meant Erik either needed money or was really in trouble. Maybe both. She felt some alarm, but a glance at his face showed he was angry.

He greeted her in a brusque manner. "You sure took your time getting home tonight, Brooke!"

"I've got a lot on my mind," she answered, fumbling with her purse for the keys.

"Yeah, I'll bet!" he snorted. "Always thinking of yourself, aren't you?"

She opened the outside door and studied her brother as he entered the hallway. He did not sound drunk and his eyes didn't seem dilated.

"What is it this time, Erik?" she asked as they climbed the carpeted stairs together.

"I need some money."

"Again?"

"Yes, again!" He stopped and faced her on the stairs. He was angry, but Brooke could also see fright in his eyes.

"It'll just be a loan, Brooke."

"Like all the others?"

"OK, if you won't help me, I'll have to get it from someone else." He led the way up the stairs again.

Brooke knew he couldn't borrow from anyone else. He had no credit rating, and he had already asked his parents for several loans over and above the money they gave him for living expenses.

"You tell me what it's for," Brooke said, unlocking the apartment door at the head of the stairs, "and I'll consider whether or not to advance you any more."

Erik entered the apartment ahead of her and flopped heavily on the couch. "Can't do that, Brooke."

"Why not?"

"Just can't, that's all. What's the big deal anyway? You never asked me what I was going to do with those other loans. How come this time is different? Now, do I get the money or not?" Erik continued when Brooke didn't answer.

Brooke voiced a few more objections, but finally gave him all the money she had in her purse. He stuffed the bills in his pants pocket and immediately stood up. At the door, he turned. "You still got problems over your tv show?"

She nodded, moving into the tiny kitchenette. "Still got them. But I'll come up with something."

"Good ol' Brooke! Always the positive thinker! Always in there, fighting to the end! Never say die and all that! Just like your old man!"

Brooke bit her tongue but said nothing. She'd heard all this many times before. She opened the refrigerator and considered what she could fix for a late snack.

Her brother's tone softened. "Anything I can do, sis?"

Brooke looked up. She was touched by his seeming concern. But as she studied his eyes, she wondered if he wasn't actually enjoying her discomfort.

He's the one that always fails, she thought. *Maybe he's hoping I'll get a dose of what it feels like.*

"Thanks anyway, Erik. But there's really nothing you can do."

He shrugged and took hold of the doorknob.

"Good night, Brooke," he finally said, and left.

Brooke stood looking at the closed door. Erik was definitely in over his head this time. She just hoped he wouldn't drown. Brooke shook off her thoughts and turned to the refrigerator. She stared into the cold interior a long time before realizing she wasn't seeing a thing; she was just thinking of how to save her job.

Once again she thought of the doctor with the fancy sports car. He looked like the type who just might bring some kind of action against her. That's all she needed!

Doctor Gregory Cameron was waiting for

Brooke the next afternoon at the garage elevator beneath the KBRG studios when she squealed into her parking place. He managed a slightly crooked grin as she walked rapidly toward the elevator.

"I see you haven't learned anything since our previous encounter, Miss Winter."

She almost missed the slight emphasis he put on her name. "Summers," she corrected him with a trace of a smile. "Brooke Summers."

He punched the elevator button for her. "Since we're not meeting professionally, I prefer to use your real name."

Brooke met his gaze steadily while she fought an urge to give a sharp retort. So he knew about her father. That meant he'd been checking up on her. Why couldn't she just be herself, instead of Senator Jak Winter's daughter? Or the daughter of the former Hollywood starlet, Beth Small, who'd married Jak Winter while he was a successful attorney. She remembered how all during high school and college she had been labeled as the daughter of the Senate majority leader.

Carefully controlling her voice, Brooke said, "Really, Mr. Cameron. . . ."

"Doctor . . . Cameron."

She stepped into the elevator when the doors slid open and suppressed a short, angry response. "Doctor Cameron, do you intend to follow me into the studio to make a scene?"

He looked down at her from his six feet, two inches, ignoring the lock of dark curly hair that fell over his right eye. It was the deepest brown eye Brooke had ever seen. He wore a light blue shirt of expensive cut; a gold medallion moved

brightly against his well-muscled neck as he
turned his head.

"Look, Miss Brooke Winter—or Summers or
whatever you want to call yourself today—I just
want my car repaired. That's all. So give me the
name of your insurance carrier, and I'll file a
claim for three hundred dollars. Then I'll get
out of your life."

"Three hundred . . . ?" Brooke exploded as the
elevator shot smoothly upward. "For that little
bitty ding? You've got to be out of your mind!"

The brown eyes turned black with anger.
"That 'little bitty ding,' as you so quaintly put it,
was on a very expensive sports car. . . . If we
settle it right here and now, I'll forget that you
left the scene of an accident without showing
me your driver's license—or giving me the other
data I'm entitled to."

Brooke wanted to lash out in self-defense, but
she also knew the elevator door would be sliding open momentarily. She didn't want a scene
in front of the KBRG staff, especially if Hal
Humphries was present.

"I'd rather pay the $300.00 than file an insur-
ance report for such a minor scrape," Brooke
answered quickly. The money would deplete
the small savings account she had, but it was
better than filing another accident report to the
insurance company. Her rates had already
been raised because of two previous accidents.

"Will you take a check?" she asked him as the
elevator bumped to a stop.

"Sure, since I know where to find you if it
bounces!"

Brooke opened her mouth to snap at him, but
bit off the words before they formed. The

elevator door slid open, and Brooke glimpsed the security guard at his desk. Quickly she reached out a long, slender forefinger and punched the *G* button. The door slid silently closed and the elevator started down.

"I'll write it for you in the garage, Dr. Cameron."

He nodded. She was aware his eyes were on her face as she dug in her purse for her checkbook. She could feel his gaze touching her lightly, skimming, darting along her neck, her shoulders. Her anger mixed with a strange swirl of pleasure.

Brooke covered her feelings by briskly stepping into the garage. She supported the small book against the side of the elevator as she scrawled her signature.

Wonder where he parked his car? she thought. *Oh, I see! Over there where I couldn't possibly clip him! He's got a lot of nerve! Why on earth am I feeling so flustered? I know his eyes are moving, moving . . .*

"There!" She turned and delivered the check with a flourish. "I trust that's the last time it'll be necessary for us to meet!"

She said it with more intensity than she intended. But nothing was going right for her. If her contract wasn't renewed, and Erik didn't start repaying her, it wouldn't be long . . .

"Thanks." Doctor Cameron took the check with his right hand and reached into his left, rear pants pocket with his free hand. He extracted a thin, brown wallet and flipped it open. A color photograph fluttered to the concrete garage floor.

Quickly Dr. Cameron bent and retrieved it.

But Brooke had seen enough that her right hand instinctively stopped him from putting the picture away.

It was obviously a "before-and-after" photograph. In the top shot, a little dark-skinned girl's face was marred by a monstrous irregular growth of flesh above her mouth. Brooke guessed the child had an enlarged cleft palate.

"How awful!" Brooke exclaimed softly.

The doctor's dark features softened. "Other kids used to call her 'pigface,' and adults referred to her as 'the little pig girl.' "

"How long did she . . . how long was she like that?" Brooke asked, tapping the top photograph.

"Ten years or so. Hard to say exactly. Her village in the Baja area of Mexico didn't have church or baptismal records, and her parents were dead."

"She was an orphan?"

"Yes."

Slowly, the realization seeped into Brooke's mind. She raised her hazel eyes until they met his dark ones. "You operated for . . .?"

"Yes." They both looked at the lower photograph: only a thickened upper lip and a hairline scar marked the child's lovely face. Greg Cameron put the picture into his wallet and snapped it shut. "Thanks for the check."

She watched him walk away. Strange! For a moment, the flash of anger in his eyes had dissipated and she had caught a glimpse of compassion. She sighed for reasons that weren't quite clear to her and pushed the elevator button.

All afternoon she purposely avoided Hal Humphries. There had been no time to research a sensational series, and she knew he would expect an answer the next time he saw her. At four o'clock he caught her coming back from a quick break.

"Hey, Summers," he called to keep her from entering her office. Slowly she turned to face the ND.

"Time's running out on you," he said, after a few words of greeting. "You'd better have something that'll hype those ratings before this day's over, or you won't have time to shoot the footage and get the stories on the air."

Brooke hesitated. Her eyes were filled with the image of that little girl's gross features before the surgery that had made her almost normal.

"Hal," Brooke said softly, feeling the emotion the picture had loosened inside her, "I've got a winner."

She was "winging it." She was "selling" the idea. Her voice was low and calm. And very self-assured.

"Yeah?" The ND sounded skeptical, but he was intrigued. His job ultimately depended on how well his news team did against brutal, unrelenting competition. "Try it on me, Brooke."

"How about a program called, 'Heartbeat'? It's an emotional segment of the news, which features warm and stirring true-life stories?"

Hal Humphries pursed his fat lips and ran the cigarette-stained forefinger over the tip of his nose.

"Such as?"

"Such as," Brooke said, thinking quickly, "a pretty little girl who was born with such a monstrous cleft palate that the kids called her 'pig face,' until a plastic surgeon donated his services to make her normal."

The thick lips spread slightly apart. The forefinger slid off the nose and dug for a pack of cigarettes. "You may have something there, Brooke. But doctors can't admit to that kind of compassion, or everyone would be after them—."

She interrupted. "This isn't the doctor's story, Hal! This is the child's! This is the story of people—all kinds of people—who had something happen to them, something which will make 'Heartbeat' viewers reach for the Kleenex."

The ND made a quick decision. "OK, shoot some footage and let's see what develops. You may get that contract renewed yet. But," Hal threatened as he shuffled off down the hallway, "it'd better be good or you'll be standing in the unemployment line!"

Chapter Four

Try as she could, Brooke couldn't come up with a suitable list of subjects which would give her a first-class audition for Heartbeat. She had plenty of possible ideas, but none that was a sure winner. And that she had to have, Brooke knew. For if Hal Humphries didn't like her first tape, there wouldn't be a second.

She was still trying ideas in her mind the next afternoon when the assignment editor called her into his office. Dick Derr was a thin, almost emaciated-looking man of about thirty. Secure in his ability to maintain a solid image of respectability, he dared to wear tennis shoes and blue jeans.

"What've you got, Dick?" Brooke asked, taking the upholstered chair he indicated from behind his battered metal desk.

"Remote with a guy who keeps poisonous

snakes in his home," he said with a grin.

Brooke shuddered. "Count me out, Dick! I hate those slithery things."

The assignment editor's brown eyes hardened. "You refusing an assignment, Brooke?"

She threw up her hands in mock horror. "Oh, no you don't! I know the surest way to get fired around a tv newsroom is to refuse an assignment. But I'm serving notice right now that I want zoom cameras and an interview with me standing outside the house. All snakes will be *inside*."

The assignment editor chuckled. "Well, in that case, I'll confess I was joking. Just testing you."

"Joking! Dick Derr, you've got a real mean streak!"

"That's why they gave me this position. Now I'll tell you the real scoop. You know all these jokers?" He pointed to the men who could be seen through the glass partition walking toward his office.

Brooke nodded. Scotty was first, suggesting a flying assignment on which he'd be the pilot. Next came Jeff Shaker, dressed sharply to resemble the on-camera tv personality he hoped to become. At present he was part of a remote crew. His job was sound man or technician. He usually carried a "deck"—a forty-pound tape recorder, which hung over his shoulders. The unit used a three-quarter-inch video cassette, which could be erased and reused, whereas film could only be used once.

Pepe Martinez was a bilingual *Latino* cameraman. He arrived in the assignment editor's office with a shoulder-mounted camera and all the accoutrements, which meant nothing to Brooke, but which she knew were part of his occupation. He was barely five-six, so Brooke stood well above him. Pepe was ambitious, like Jeff, but quieter and more traditionally dressed in faded blue jeans, polo shirt, and blue jogging shoes.

"Now," Dick Derr began, "since we're all here, let's get down to basics. First off, I could have brought in an engineer and a reporter on this caper, but why run up the price tag and ruin my budget when you three have worked so well together before? Brooke, you're the reporter. Scotty, you've already been told to rent a fixed-wing aircraft and have it standing by."

Scotty nodded.

Then Dick Derr turned to Jeff and Pepe. "You two know your jobs. Now, this assignment will require some tact and a lot of care."

Brooke interrupted, "Nothing scary like a house full of pet snakes, is it, Dick?"

"No, not this time. We've set things up for you to do a 'shoot' on some marijuana fields about one hundred miles upstate. Humphries thinks it might be a good kickoff for a series on San Francisco's drug racket."

"Hey!" Jeff protested, "that could be dangerous! Feds on one hand, the growers on the other, and us the edible part in between."

"Exactly," the assignment editor agreed. "But if you play the cards right, nobody'll get hurt, and you'll get a story on *san semilla* that'll maybe win this station some big ratings, maybe an award for you, Brooke. . . . Sorry about you two guys."

Pepe smiled, showing a wide expanse of white

teeth. "I don't want you to worry! *San semilla* means 'without seeds,' and is the finest type of marijuana grown. I will have my reward on this trip."

Dick Derr shook his head. "None of that! I don't want the station in trouble. Just do a nice, clean 'shoot,' and get home with the film. Is that clear?"

The television crew nodded. Personally, Brooke found the assignment distasteful. There had been rumors that marijuana was being grown in vast quantities in the northern forested area of California. Where there was that much big money, there was certain to be crime and trouble. But an assignment was an assignment. Brooke shrugged and walked down to the elevator with the three men.

There Jeff snapped his fingers. "Whoops! Forgot something. Be right back!" He turned away.

Scotty called after him. "I've got to file a flight plan and some other things. We'll go on ahead and meet you at the airport. You know which hangar."

Pepe said, "I'll wait and ride with Jeff. You two go ahead. OK?"

Brooke and Scotty exchanged glances. Scotty smiled. "Why not? Come on, Brooke, let's get moving."

She was glad for the change in plans, which allowed her to be alone with Scotty in his car. She wanted to tell him about Heartbeat. They were barely seated and backing out of the underground parking lot when Brooke brought up the subject.

Scotty listened in silence, keeping his eyes on

the road. He had always contended that flying was much safer than driving through the over-crowded streets of San Francisco. But when Brooke had finished telling Scotty the whole story, he impulsively reached across the front seat and squeezed her left hand.

"Brooke, it's great! Really great! Heartbeat is a sure winner!"

"Thanks, Scotty! Coming from you, I know you really mean it. But I still don't have a solid idea for the audition film."

"You open to suggestions?" He didn't let go of her hand.

"That's why I mentioned it to you."

Scotty freed Brooke's hand to gesture with his right forefinger. "Then fly with me to Baja California Sur, about six hundred miles below the Mexican border. There's an orphanage there with a million heartaches—or Heartbeats! I frequently fly Christian doctors, nurses, dentists, and others down there for weekend clinics.

"You could fly with us Labor Day weekend in a light plane caravan and get some great footage! Your job would be secure; you'd surely bring up the ratings with a series of feature stories from there, and besides, I'd get you all to myself—at least—for a few days. What'd you say?"

Baja again! Why did that name keep popping up? First, Dr. Cameron's little pig girl. Now a story for Heartbeat. Mexico held too many bad memories for her to return willfully.

She explained to Scotty. "Ten years ago I traveled to several towns south of Tijuana with some kids from my high school Spanish class. I nearly died down there. I mean it—nearly died. Sure, we knew not to drink the water, and we were really careful about what we ate, but I came down with something. For two days I wore a path in the carpet between my hotel bed and the bathroom. Then, when I broke out in a high fever, they put me in this dingy concrete hospital room.

"I don't remember much about the next few days except that they kept giving me shots, and my insides felt like they were going to explode. I thought only people in the jungles of Africa got typhoid fever, but that's what the doctor said I had. Finally, after about two weeks in that awful hospital, I was well enough to go home. . . . But I didn't feel like doing much of anything for a couple of months.

"I vowed, 'never again,' and I've stuck to that. Only a person who had been really sick down there can appreciate how serious it can be; none of those 'Montezuma's Revenge' jokes for me!"

Scotty listened patiently. When she was finished, he took his eyes off the road long enough to protest, "But this is different! We'll fly straight there, carrying all our own food and water; we'll let the doctors do their thing; and then we'll fly back before you can even get close to a germ."

"Scotty, I just can't!"

"Besides," he ignored her protest, "there's got to be some great footage there. Like the time I saw a six-year-old girl taking care of her four-year-old brother; just the two of them living in a rag tent with nobody to look out for them. Some missionaries decided to start an orphanage there, and the governor of Baja California Sur heard about it; he personally asked to turn the first spade of dirt at the groundbreaking. The state donated ten acres of land and volunteers from California churches flew down for a long weekend or working vacation to build the place."

"Scotty . . ."

"Tell you what, I'll say a special prayer that you won't get sick, and that you come out with the best story of your life. How about that?"

"You get guarantees with your prayers, Scotty?"

His face sobered. "Not that, exactly. But I believe everything works out for those who are trying to seek God's will."

Brooke sighed, looking ahead at the freeway, which they'd entered. "I don't know," she said, "If anything should happen again . . ."

"I don't want to talk you into it, Brooke, but it can't be any more dangerous than this illegal drug story. Frankly, I don't like this assignment at all.

"But to fly down to Baja, clear to Guerrero Negro in a day, and then back within seventy-two hours . . ." He left the sentence unfinished.

"Guerrero Negro?"

"Translates as Black Warrior. Fascinating place. Want me to give you some reading material to bone up on?"

"Now wait a minute. I haven't said I'd go."

"OK. Speaking of going, we're short one doctor. The physician who was going had to cancel out. Know where I can recruit a volunteer?"

Brooke's head jerked around so she looked full at Scotty's profile. Maybe . . . ?

The car's two-way radio squawked. Scotty picked up the microphone with his right hand, drove with his left, and acknowledged the call.

The speaker on the dashboard squawked again. "Scotty, this is Jeff. Some idiot fired shots into a downtown bar. Killed four people. Pepe and I have been assigned to cover it with one of the news crew. We'll have to wait for the cops to discover another marijuana field. Do you read me?"

"Loud and clear, Jeff, thanks! Trip canceled. We'll return to the studio soon as possible."

Scotty replaced the microphone and muttered, "Thanks, Lord!"

"Amen," Brooke added and was surprised at herself. She was glad this trip was finished before it began. But what about Heartbeat and Baja?

Chapter Five

Brooke's mind was racing as she made final preparations for the "Six O'Clock News Report" that night. Humphries had "bought" her idea; now she had to come up with something quickly. The logical thing would be to ask Greg Cameron about the little girl who had the severe cleft palate. But he had come and gone, and Brooke had no intention of risking another conflict-filled scene with him. No, she concluded, she would have to come up with something on her own.

Automatically, Brooke removed her Channel Three blazer to drop the IFB (intermittent feedback) cord across her shoulders. She slipped the tiny unit into her ear so the producer could talk to her on the air if necessary. The earplug didn't show when Brooke's hair was allowed to fall naturally into position

Next, she put her blazer back on over the trailing cord so it was also invisible to the camera. She took her place before the cameras and went over some notes she had scribbled as the camera operators focused the large empty lenses.

Two of the operators were *Latinos*. Both wore white T-shirts, blue jeans, and tennis shoes. Another was an avowed homosexual who preferred to be known as "gay." The fourth camera operator was a young white girl in baggy pants and a man's unironed blue work shirt. The TelePrompTer operator was also a white female.

The floor director walked in front of the cameras and curled his nose slightly at Brooke. Brooke ignored him as he barked out occasional orders to both his production people and Brooke. The news department traditionally didn't get along with the production staff and Brooke's lack of response was her way of acting out the feud. The crew especially considered the anchorwoman to be an object of contempt. If Brooke complained too much about anything, they'd air some bad angles of her under the guise of "an accident." It wasn't that Brooke didn't try to get along with everyone; it was just the nature of the giant corporate structure to envy the successful, especially those who had achieved so much at such a young age.

Brooke's mind snapped off her own private thoughts when she heard the quiet voice, "The floor is ready."

She licked her lips and forced a smile. The network monitor behind the cameras and Tele-PrompTer showed the wind-up of the program that preceded the news.

" 'The Six O'Clock News' is next," the announcer said as a commercial followed.

Brooke was a veteran of the evening newscasts, but her nerves still stood on edge in these last few minutes before air time. The floor director knelt between cameras one and two, his headset trailing a long black cord. "Fifteen seconds. . . . Stand by."

The floor director's hands went up. Seven fingers showed. The two on the left hand curled down, then the five fingers on the right—quickly, smoothly, second by second. The floor director held first and second fingers together on his right hand and swept them silently and meaningfully toward camera two. The red light winked mutely atop it. Brooke looked directly into the live camera and began reading from the TelePrompTer as it began to roll.

"Good evening! I'm Brooke Summers, and this is the 'Six O'Clock News Report.' Here are today's top stories."

She read the copy smoothly and easily, almost as if she had it memorized. At least that's how it appeared to the Channel Three viewers. Actually, Brooke was watching the words come up on the TelePrompTer. The introductions over, the first videotape rolled.

In all, Brooke was on the air eight minutes during the entire hour. Then the last red camera light winked silently out, and the hot overhead lights were turned off. Jerry Hansen, the weatherman, stood off to Brooke's left and began erasing his elaborate blackboard as the floor crew began to pull the cameras away from the set. Brooke started to remove the IFB earpiece when it clicked slightly in her ear.

"Hey, Brooke, the news director wants to see you in his office right away."

Brooke nodded toward the control room in the corner of the studio and removed her blazer. She unhooked her cable and laid the unit down on her chair. *Now what?* she wondered as she walked toward Hal Humphries's office. She knocked on the door and entered at the news director's brusque invitation. Hal Humphries jabbed his cigarette into an ashtray on his desk and waved Brooke to a seat. He leaned back in his high-backed swivel chair, laced both hands across his flabby paunch, and squinted at his newscaster. His eyes were fixed on her, as if he were searching for an answer.

"Brooke, if you didn't have the reputation of being the newsroom's resident ice virgin, I'd say you'd been playing up to the Old Man."

"Never met him," Brooke answered, sitting and crossing her long legs to give an impression of casualness. She had no idea what was going on, but bluff was part of the corporate game. She'd listen and wait.

Humphries frowned. "You sure you never met him?"

"The company president? Never seen him."

The news director snorted, pursing his thick lips thoughtfully. "Yeah; well, anyway, he's apparently noticed you. Not that I can blame him on that score."

Hal paused a moment, then spoke again. "The Old Man's taken an interest in things philanthropic. Who knows why? Anyway, he's sent word that he wants you to represent KBRG on one of his pet projects."

"On my own time?"

"Of course. You secure enough in your position to turn down a request to do some goody-goody work for the man who signs your paycheck?"

Brooke sighed softly. "OK. I get the picture. What kind of a philanthropic project am I volunteering for?"

"There's an advisory board being formed to help build a new hospital wing for North Bay University. Media people are always welcome on such things."

"How often does it meet?"

"I don't know. But here's the name of the chairman. Give him a call."

Brooke glanced at the card. It was a simple business card with black letters, neat and discreet. But the name in the center leaped up at her: Gregory T. Cameron, M.D.

Questions chased each other through Brooke's mind as she made her way to her office. The police radio was turned down to a respectable level. The station monitor was on, but the sound was down, too. She switched on her desk lamp and sat down, examining the card in her hands.

Had the Old Man really assigned her to this venture, or had Dr. Cameron somehow arranged it? And why was she so excited by the prospect of seeing the dominant doctor again.

Her phone rang, startling Brooke so much she involuntarily jerked. She picked it up, half-expecting to hear Greg Cameron's voice. Instead, it was her brother.

"Brooke, I've got to see you right after the 'Eleven O'Clock News.'"

Ordinarily, she'd have argued or made an excuse. But there was the waver of panic in his tone. "All right," she said quietly. "Where?"

"Top-of-the-City. Don't be late."

Brooke finished her final newscast, changed into street clothes but didn't stop to remove her makeup, and headed for the famous San Francisco restaurant. As she stepped out of the elevator, she automatically looked at the splendid sight below her, which was visible through the extensive glass windows.

The City (as it was respectfully called, never "Frisco") was spread out in a spangled display of lights. Brooke could even see beyond to the lights of private yachts and commercial ships, which dotted the dark expanse of San Francisco Bay. Brooke still thought it was the most beautiful city in the world. But tonight Brooke's mind was on her brother. She scanned the crowd at the bar first because that's where she thought he'd be. Then she spotted him, seated alone at a side window table. She slid into the chair opposite him and was surprised to see he had ordered a soft drink.

"What is it, Erik?"

His eyes skittered around the softly lit room designed to suggest the romantic atmosphere of the good life. He turned his attention to his glass, avoiding Brooke's anxious eyes.

"I'm in big trouble, sis."

"Erik, if you're going to ask for more money—"

"How about one of your credit cards?"

"No! You know I'm already up to my ears in debt because of the things I've bought with plastic!"

"Come on, Brooke! Just one! What about an airline credit card?"

Brooke was alarmed. "Why do you need an airline ticket?"

Her brother shrugged and rattled the ice in his glass. "I miscalculated and need to get away for a while."

She kept her voice low. "What do you mean miscalculated?"

"It doesn't matter. Yes or no—will you give me the card?"

"No! And it does matter! C'mon, Erik, will you please tell me what happened?"

He glanced around the room, lowered his voice, and leaned across the table. "I had a piece of the action in a marijuana field up the coast. Only it got raided today." He stopped.

"And you figure the bust will eventually lead to you. Erik! How could you? What'll dad say?"

Erik swore and set his drink down so hard people turned to stare. "Never mind about him! What about me?"

"Erik! Please! Don't make a scene!"

He pushed his hands down hard on the table and shoved himself to his feet. He towered angrily over Brooke, fear making his voice tremble. "Yes or no, Brooke? That's all I want to know!"

Brooke glanced around. The clink of glasses and pleasant late-night conversation was stilled. Those who were not directly staring at Erik and Brooke were obviously listening. Brooke reached out an imploring hand to her brother, but he brushed it away.

Brooke didn't see the tall, dark man approach. He was just there, standing beside her. For a moment, she didn't recognize Dr. Cameron because he wore a conservative gray suit.

Then he spoke in a very low, but firm, tone.

"Miss Summers, is there anything I can do?"

Erik turned to face him. Before Brooke could reply, Erik snapped, "Yes! You can get the blazes out of here! This is none of your business."

"It is now."

Brooke slid to her feet to come between the two men, but she accidentally collided with a tall, striking blonde woman. She was perfectly dressed in a green sheath, which picked up the hue of her eyes.

"Oops!" Brooke said, "I'm sorry."

"It's all right, honey," the woman replied in a low, throaty voice. Brooke suspected the blond deliberately cultivated her lower octive to imitate some screen sex symbol. Brooke had already turned to her brother and the doctor when the woman's words came softly to her. "Sometimes it takes a long time to grow up to be graceful, my dear."

Brooke shot a disbelieving glance at the speaker, but shook off the slur and stood between the two angry men. She kept her voice low.

"Please, both of you! They'll throw us all out of here in a minute. Everyone sit down, please!"

"Who's he?" Erik demanded of Brooke.

"Who're you?" Greg Cameron snapped back.

"Me?" Erik blazed. "I'm her brother, that's who!"

"Oh." The doctor's voice was still low, but it had lost some of it's stiffness. "Well, that's still no reason to make a scene in a public place."

Out of the corner of her eye, Brooke could see male employees moving discreetly, but purposefully toward her group. "Please, Dr. Cameron! I can handle things. Come on, Erik. Let's get out of here!"

For a moment, Erik glowered at Dr. Cameron, only to find the physician returning stare for stare. Then Erik's eyes dropped. He coughed nervously and tried to smile at his sister.

"Brooke, that's the first one of your boyfriends who didn't back down from me."

Brooke stiffened. She was surprised to see the throaty-voiced blond do the same. Instantly, Brooke guessed that this striking, green-eyed beauty was Dr. Cameron's date. Brooke was surprised to find that she resented the woman standing so close to the handsome doctor.

The management team moved discreetly into the scene, silencing the antagonists by their presence.

Brooke felt her brother lightly touch her arm. "So long, sis." He pushed his way into the crowd and was lost to sight.

Embarrassed, Brooke lifted her eyes to Dr. Greg Cameron. "I'm sorry," she said. "But thank you." She thought of adding some brief explanation about her brother's behavior, but decided against it. Her eyes went unwillingly to the blond. Brooke found herself terribly unsure of what to say or do.

The doctor came to her rescue. "Miss Brooke Summers, Miss Cynthia Langdon."

"You must excuse us," the blond said, wrapping her smooth, bare arm through Greg's arm. Cynthia smiled but as she turned toward Greg Brooke caught a nasty, disapproving look. The couple would probably argue over Greg's involvement in her domestic squabble. Brooke was surprised to find herself hoping it was a good fight, one that might break up their relationship.

Suddenly, Brooke was aware that people were staring at her. Some undoubtedly recognized her. She paid her brother's small bill and hurried to the elevators. The lights above one elevator were going down, so she rang for the second elevator and took it to street level. But there was no sign of her brother in the lobby—or in the street outside.

Brooke was aware that Erik was in deep trouble, which might get him thrown in jail. Or even worse, maybe Erik had done something to upset the others involved in the illegal drug operation. Was there a chance his life might be in jeopardy? She had covered enough syndicate killings to know that the mob would do anything to keep someone from talking—even if that person had gotten involved innocently.

Chapter Six

Tired as she was from the awful scene at the Top-of-the-City and the pressures of her job, Brooke awoke several times during the night and finally got up when the faint rays of daybreak were beginning to lighten the sky.

Her mind zigzagged between the audition footage, which needed to be shot within the next two weeks (either right before or right after Labor Day weekend) and her brother's abrupt disappearance the night before. As early as it was she still called Erik's apartment. But there was no answer. Should she call her parents? No. They'd only worry, and there was no use waking them so early on Sunday morning. Instead she decided to get out of the apartment and go for a walk so she could think.

When she left, she was wearing a bright yellow blouse and matching skirt. Cheerful colors, she told herself, would help get her spirits back up to their usual heights. A northwesterly wind off the Pacific Ocean had made this August morning gray and cold; the sun had not yet burned through the high, dense fog to warm the day. Brooke had come to love this kind of day, typical of San Francisco, but this morning she longed for the sun—or somewhere warm where she could sit and think.

After a few blocks of aimless wandering, she saw a small, red-brick church that reminded her of the church she attended as a child. Strains of a favorite hymn, "Amazing grace, how sweet the sound," came through a small stained-glass window above the sidewalk as the choir rehearsed for the coming service. The familiar melody took her mind back to earlier years when she had delighted in her father's unabashed pride in his beautiful, intelligent little girl. She paused to listen as she thought of those long-ago days.

Brooke would have done anything to please the tall, slender man whose somber eyes lit up in a special way when she came into the room. She and her father had clashed only when Brooke was in her early teens. But her rebellion was nothing out of the ordinary for an adolescent struggling to attain identity. When Jak Winter laid down the law on curfew, or forbid his daughter to date certain boys, Brooke had screamed and threatened that she'd do as she pleased. But she never had.

The combination of her dad's discipline—and the Christian virtues instilled in her by her parents—helped her say no to drugs, sex, and many of the other vices that had gotten some of her friends in trouble in high school. Though Brooke didn't always show it, she gained a terrific amount of respect and appreciation for her father during those years. By the time Brooke went off to Stanford, she and her father were closer than ever.

Erik was just the opposite. He rarely made a scene when his father said no, but inside the seeds of rebellion had been forming. He had especially resented the pressure his dad unconsciously put upon him to succeed. Jak Winter had wanted his only son to be an outstanding athlete, president of the student council, and a straight A student. When he didn't meet his father's exceptionally high standards, Erik rebelled by using drugs and putting his studies almost completely aside.

Brooke switched her thoughts back to herself as the choir stopped practicing and people moved past her to enter the church. She wondered what kind of a parent she'd be. And more importantly, whom she would marry. Her mind flickered through the men she knew. Funny how much parents influenced a child in the choice of a mate. Brooke wanted someone like her father: kind, gentle, yet firm, intelligent, and ambitious. But Brooke wanted something else, too—something more than a good man. She wanted someone who really cared about people.

A cold breeze slapped at Brooke's cheek, sending a chill through her body. With an effort, she checked her drifting thoughts and decided to enter the church, which looked warm and inviting. She slipped in quietly, accepted a bulletin from an usher, and slid into the farthest corner of the back row on the right, near the door.

The choir filed in, their rich, wine-colored robes glistening under the overhead lights. The pastor and some assistants trailed them, taking seats in stiff, high-backed chairs as the choir started to sing. Brooke felt a warm glow fill her body as she listened to the music.

The choir finished and sat down and an assistant in a dark suit read from the Scriptures. Brooke felt the special moment of warmth begin to slip away. Her eyes began to wander over the congregation.

That's when she saw Dr. Gregory Cameron sitting one row forward and near the far end of the pew across the aisle. At first, Brooke wasn't sure it was he. She stared. He turned. Their eyes met. Neither gave any sign of recognition, but it was a long moment before she lowered her eyes.

After the service, she tried to slip out unnoticed, embarrassed by the scene at the restaurant. But Dr. Cameron had apparently anticipated her move; he was striding alongside her before she could reach the narthex exit.

"How about lunch?" he asked, taking her arm and continuing toward the outside doors.

Brooke hesitated. She had felt uncomfortable every time they had met, and yet, she still wanted to be with this imposing doctor she couldn't forget. She thought of a logical reason to have lunch with him.

"Well, it would be a good opportunity to talk about the new North Bay Hospital wing. The KBRG president recently assigned me to the board."

Greg's eyebrows went up. "You're going to

serve on my committee? Then by all means, let's have lunch and get acquainted. Let's try," he said with a wry grin, "to keep the subject off cars and brothers."

They sat at a window booth in a quiet restaurant overlooking Fisherman's Wharf. The morning fog had finally lifted, leaving a canopy of blue sky over the bay. Brightly colored boats bobbled back and forth in the gentle waves, and the soft breeze held the pleasant aroma of salt water.

"I was really surprised to see you in church," Brooke admitted as she munched on delicious sourdough bread covered with butter.

The dark eyes seemed amused. "And I was surprised when you accepted my invitation to lunch."

"Spur-of-the-moment weakness, I guess." Brooke started to take another bite of bread, then paused. "Besides, I didn't get to thank you for trying to help me last night."

"Is your brother OK?"

"I don't know. I haven't heard from him since he stomped away from the table."

"You want to talk about it?"

Brooke looked out at the peaceful scene before them. "I'm not sure."

He ran a browned hand thoughtfully across his dark chin. He'd shaved that morning, she was sure, yet there was a hint of beard already. It was part of the masculine virility she'd sensed from the start.

"I'm sure of one thing," he said. "I'd like us to forget how we met and begin to get acquainted right now.... I think we owe that to each other."

She almost smiled. It sounded like a line, yet

she thought he just might be sincere. Brooke didn't know if she could trust the searching—almost soft—look in his eyes. But he had noted the amusement that lingered in her eyes.

"You're laughing at me."

"Oh, no!"

"Not with your mouth, but with your eyes. Do you find me amusing?"

Amusing? Brooke asked herself. *No. Intriguing, yes. Mysterious, hiding some kind of a secret, one that might make you even more attractive.* Brooke could feel her emotions stirring.

"Well," he demanded, "what's your opinion of me?"

"My opinion, Dr. Cameron—"

"Greg."

"My opinion—Greg—is that I'm willing to forget we met before. That is, if you think we can get along now without fighting."

He smiled, then reached a hand across to clasp her right one. "Let's shake on it."

"That's fine with me, as long as this doesn't turn out to be like one of those all-star wrestling matches—where they shake hands and then come out fighting."

She felt his hand squeeze hers gently. "Let's shake on that, too," he said.

They had enjoyed their light, almost meaningless, conversation so much (he was one of the few people who could answer her quips and then quickly return another) that the dessert was served before Brooke brought up the new wing for North Bay Hospital. But Greg Cameron steadfastly refused to discuss his work, his family, or his background.

"It's too beautiful a day to talk about such

things," he said and deftly slanted the conversation toward her so that Brooke told him about her family and the new Heartbeat series she was contemplating for the news.

Hours later as she stood on the beach looking out toward the Farallone Islands, she realized she knew little about him even though he had learned a lot about her. Greg had offered to take her home, but she had insisted that he let her off at the beach so she could enjoy the late afternoon sun and the refreshing cool water on her feet. If he hadn't promised to check on a postoperative patient, she was sure he would have stayed with her.

Greg Cameron is a strange man, she thought as she walked along the water's edge, carrying her shoes in her hand. He could be egotistical, loud, demanding, even belligerent—yet other times he was subdued: assured, gentle, and mysterious.

Scotty grinned at Brooke from the side of the elevator as she whipped her red Cutlass into her parking place under Channel Three studios the next day.

"I'd hoped you'd slowed up by now, Brooke,' he said, walking to meet her.

"Hello, Scotty." She smiled and he fell into step beside her.

"That plane caravan I told you about i: scheduled to leave next Friday for Baja. The long Labor Day weekend makes it easier fo those of us with jobs to get away. You decided t come along?"

Brooke was tempted. She needed that audi tion footage shot soon, but she still didn't lik going back to Baja. Not after her first and only trip. It didn't matter that thousands of other people went there without incident.

"Scotty, I just don't know. Let me think about it a little longer." She smiled at him as she stepped out of the elevator and waved good-bye as the doors closed behind her.

When she got to her office, a note to call Hal Humphries had been attached to her desk lamp where she'd be bound to see it. Reluctantly Brooke dialed his office, trying to sound confident as she said, "Brooke returning your call, Hal."

"Oh, yeah; thanks. I got a call from the 'Old Man.' He says your regular segment is looking better, but the rating period is coming up, and he wants us to look good. How you doing on that Heartbeat idea?"

"I'm working on it, Hal."

"Any ideas?"

Brooke pondered a second. "Well, yes; there's an opportunity to fly down to an orphanage in Baja next weekend with a caravan of doctors and nurses."

"Orphans are always good copy, Brooke. You going to do it?"

"I had an awful experience down there once. I'd really like to come up with something else."

"OK. Take a couple days. But if you don't have something by then, you'd better head for Baja."

Chapter Seven

Brooke closed her eyes while the makeup was applied. "You understand, Scotty," she said with her eyes still closed, "I'm only going to do it as a last resort."

His voice came from across the room where he was sitting in a battered old easy chair. "I'm going to go ahead just as though it's an assignment. I'll have to work out the final details on the border crossing. Too bad we can't take the private jet, but the caravan of light planes is better. Less of *la mordida*."

The makeup man's fingers moved away from Brooke's eyes and a light brush was applied to her nose. Brooke opened her eyes and looked at Scotty. *"La mordida?* What's that?"

He grinned. "The bite. Old cultural habit south of the border."

"You mean, 'bribe'?"

The pilot threw up his hands in mock horror. "What a crude suggestion! No, it's just the way things are done! You want something, you pay for it. But when you get to the next official, he is 'soo sorry, but these ees the wrong paper, *Senor!* You must have these kind, which I have.' And so *la mordida* again."

"You're kidding?"

"Not at all. Most Mexican government employees are paid average to below-average wages. It's their unofficial way of supplementing their income. They see it as 'paying tolls as you go.'"

"I'm fascinated, Scotty! That might make a good feature itself."

He shook his head. "Good neighbors don't talk unkindly about officials of bordering countries; not on tv. You wouldn't want to create an international incident, would you?"

"Not me!" Brooke looked in the hand mirror the makeup man handed her. Brooke was satisfied. The protective bib was removed. "I've got enough problems without getting involved in something like that."

"Good! You won't need a passport, but you'd better have a secretary get you a tourist card from the Mexican Government Tourism Department or the Mexican Consulate. Sometimes they don't ask for them across the border, but there's no sense getting turned back. The card is free."

Brooke looked in the large, dressing room mirror, and began straightening her blouse. "I'm not too keen on those light planes, Scotty. I've covered too many crashes."

The pilot looked at her eyes in the mirror.

"We don't have much choice. There are no real airports where we're going, and piston aircraft's the only thing for such conditions. Besides, you'll get such good shots that you'll be glad you went."

"Scotty. . . ."

"OK! OK! But wait'll you see those kids in that orphanage. It's sure a vast improvement over the first facility I saw down there. Did I ever tell you about that one?"

"No, but I'm not sure I want to hear about it."

"You need to know, so you can see the vast improvement that has been made." Scotty rushed on to keep Brooke from objecting. "There were a lot of boys running around, seemingly wild. They were dirty, their lips were chapped, and large bug bites marred their faces. Someone had cropped their hair short to help control lice."

"Really, Scotty. . . ."

"They had no socks or underwear. At night, some of them wore two pair of pants to keep warm—at least those who had two pair of pants. I'll never forget a couple of those kids who just stood and screamed because they had some kind of an ear disease.

"If we played too much with the younger boys, the bigger ones got jealous and hit the smaller ones. All of those kids were starving for attention; they'd do almost anything for it. Like a little guy called Lalo. He was maybe five years old and looked like a sumo wrestler. He grinned sideways while his mouth spewed forth some of the most vulgar obscenities I've ever heard. It was his way of getting noticed."

"Oh, Scotty. . . ."

"The place smelled really bad. Four of the six toilets were stopped up and there was no toilet paper. Inside the boys' rooms, there was a special all-purpose bucket, which they used for a toilet so they wouldn't have to go down the hall."

"Scotty, enough!"

"You really should know it all, Brooke," Scotty answered as he continued on. "I saw one tub and one shower, but I'll bet they didn't work. And it was never quiet: there were roosters crowing, dogs barking, and people shouting. The big kids cooked. I don't think any of the kids brushed their teeth or went to school. . . . Every time I remember that place, I want to cry. We got to leave, but they couldn't."

"I am not going to get emotionally involved with those children, Scotty. I just want to get my story and get out, *pronto*. That is, if I go at all," Brooke reminded him as she got up, and they walked into the large studio.

"I'm still hoping I'll come up with something else. Like maybe a scoop at the hospital board meeting tomorrow night," she laughed sarcastically, knowing that the probability was minuscule—if not totally impossible.

Brooke began hooking up her cables for the program. "See you later, Scotty."

He winked knowingly and turned away. Brooke continued to prepare for her telecast sensing that Scotty was probably right: Her Labor Day vacation would be spent working in Baja, of all places.

The board meeting was held in a small, oblong room. A dozen swivel, tilt-back, upholstered chairs lined a glistening mahogany table in the room's center. In the corner, stood a small cart with several Styrofoam cups ringing a silver-and-black carafe of coffee.

Brooke was introduced to everyone, but the only name she remembered was one she already knew: Dr. Gregory Cameron. He had greeted her with a casual "Hello," and showed no outward sign of any feeling toward her except when he offered his right hand. She had felt a slight, extra squeeze on her fingers.

Brooke had expected Greg Cameron to chair the meeting. But he moved quickly through the preliminaries and then turned the floor over to a cherubic doctor who had retired a year ago. It didn't take Brooke long to see that the man enjoyed throwing his weight around. Greg sat back and said almost nothing as the evening progressed.

The meeting was fairly routine for a couple of hours as the objectives were outlined and discussed. Even Brooke found them admirable. There was need for a new building at the old North Bay University Hospital, primarily to house a much expanded pediatric program. Statistics proved the need. But it was the strategy that sparked Brooke's disagreement.

"Excuse me," she said, "did I understand that you purpose to have a press conference and invite all the media to help kick off this fund drive?"

The meeting chairman nodded. "Do you find that objectionable?" the older doctor asked peering over his funny-looking reading glasses.

Of course it was unfair. What was the purpose of Brooke's sitting on one of these boards, or her own time, unless there was some benefit

She felt she had a legitimate right to get a head start on the competition. But she didn't dare say that.

"I would appreciate it," she commented, smiling and trying to be considerate, "if someone from the board would appear live on our Channel Three 'News Report' the night before the press conference to explain your plans."

There were some questions by other board members. They were generally for the idea, but agreed it wasn't a good idea to play favorites with the media.

Doctor Gregory Cameron spoke for the first time since he'd relinquished the chair. "I think this board is overlooking the obvious. Miss Summers has consented to serve on this board, without compensation, as do all of us, and on her own time. I believe she is suggesting that it would be appropriate to give her an advantage. I believe the old-fashioned word—if it applies to television as well as newspapers—is a 'scoop.' "

Brooke was flustered. There was nothing about a routine board meeting that was even remotely worthy of what he'd called a "scoop," but she couldn't say that. For some reason, Channel Three's president had taken a liking to this board and its objectives. Brooke wasn't about to say something which might be politically damaging to the "Old Man."

"I simply made a suggestion, gentlemen. I don't see how it could harm this board to consider it for what it is: an offer to help through early media exposure."

"I fully understand Miss Summer's rationale," Greg Cameron acknowledged.

"However, I don't favor supporting it."

Brooke blinked in surprise. She had been sure he was on her side. Well, she didn't need him!

"I merely made a suggestion to the board," she answered quietly.

"Then," Dr. Cameron said, "if the chair will entertain a motion, I move that the board treat all media alike. The press conference will be the first public announcement of our plans."

There was some discussion before the board voted to follow Greg Cameron's suggestion, which he had restated as a formal motion. Brooke was seething inside as she forced a smile and said good night to each board member. She wanted to leave immediately, but felt that might look as if she were pouting. Consequently, she accepted the treasurer's suggestion to wait a moment, while he went down to the administrative offices to get a copy of the budget. When everyone had gone except Brooke and Greg, she turned her eyes upon him.

"You know, Dr. Cameron, I never cease to marvel at how some boards comprising successful and bright people fail to understand how to deal with the media."

He stood next to her beside the long table, his dark eyes somberly meeting her hazel ones. "You understand," he said a little stiffly, "that I did what I thought was best for the hospital?"

"You needn't explain your actions, Dr. Cameron."

"So you are angry?"

"Over such a little thing? Really, doctor!" She walked quickly to the coatrack in the corner and picked up her light rain jacket. She had one arm in it when she heard his quick step behind her. He helped her into the other sleeve.

"Brooke," he said softly, but strongly, "I don't want us to start fighting again."

"Oh? Then why do you go out of your way to provoke me?"

"Brooke, I really don't have time for these childish confrontations. . . ."

She whirled on him. "Childish confron . . . Good night, Dr. Cameron!"

She turned angrily but he took one quick step, caught her in strong arms, and spun her around. She glared hostilely up at him as he pulled her close. His dark eyes were black with intense emotion, but Brooke hardly noticed. She pushed her arms against his broad chest in a vain struggle to get away.

"Let me . . . go!"

"Brooke—"

"I'd scream if I thought that'd do any good! . . . But your friends would probably think I was molesting you." She was so angry the words poured out of her in a blind, pursing gush of resentment. She didn't think; she just reacted.

Suddenly, he bent and kissed her. She was too surprised to resist, and soon was aware that his lips were firm and good against hers. He was not gentle, and yet he wasn't rough, either. It was a surprise sensation, which touched her senses and sent them into erratic patterns.

He didn't say anything. He didn't even give her a chance to react after the kiss. He simply let her go as quickly as he'd seized her, turned, and pushed his way out the door and into the corridor.

Brooke stood uncertainly, her feet a little unsteady, still not knowing what she felt or thought.

She had always prided herself on being able to handle any situation and calmly reason out most problems. But as she drove home, Greg's kiss still fresh on her lips, she was utterly confused.

Something inside of her seemed to be drawn to him. It was a mysterious feeling that she had never felt before. Brooke knew that she was too angry to be falling in love with Greg Cameron, but she had to admit, the handsome doctor had been at the forefront of her thoughts. And what was that great mystical secret he seemed to be hiding? she wondered again.

Absently, Brooke parked her car and walked toward the outside entrance to her apartment building. As she unlocked the downstairs door and pushed it open, a wave of horror rolled through her body. The corner of her eye had caught a long shadow disengaging itself from the shrubbery. Brooke's hand flew to her mouth.

The man's shadow moved toward her. As Brooke hurried to slam the door she heard an intense whisper. "Brooke. It's me—Erik."

She controlled her frightened breathing and quickly moved to catch the door before it banged shut. "Erik! Where on earth have you been?"

"Shh! Let's get upstairs to your place so we can talk." He glanced nervously around.

Brooke silently turned and led the way up the stairs. As soon as they were in her apartment, her brother flopped on the couch, his legs sticking straight out as he leaned back with relief.

"Now, Brooke, before you start saying things, let me tell you I just blew town for a few days, that's all."

"You're driving me crazy; do you know that? First you stomp off into the night going who knows where, and then you nearly scare me to death." She slammed the lid down on the coffeepot and plugged the cord into the counter wall socket.

He grinned at her over his shoulder. "Nice to know somebody cares about me, sis."

"All I care about is that you stay out of trouble." She sat down on the arm of the couch that was nearest the kitchenette. "Is that clear?"

"Clear," he said. "I think I'm off the hook on that marijuana bust."

"Is that why you came back? Or do you want to borrow a credit card and get some more money?"

Her brother's eyes narrowed suspiciously. "Is all that hostility for me, or am I getting the backwash from some lover's quarrel?"

Brooke got up and turned back to the kitchen. She inspected the coffeepot, jiggling the plug to make sure it was in securely. "I'm just concerned about what happens to you, Erik. And to mom, dad, and me because of you."

She came back in and faced her brother. "When are you going to quit behaving like a teenager and face up to the responsibility of who you are and what you are?"

He stood up, his face serious. "I had a terrible scare, I'll admit. For a while there, I didn't know if I was avoiding the Feds, or the other guys involved in the action. But I think I've got the whole thing straightened out."

She thought of a quick retort but stifled it. "Did the scare do you any good?"

He shrugged and turned to inspect one of the pictures on the wall. "I don't know. I just got to thinking about the mess my life's in, and how I could've been killed in this latest caper. So, well— I went to church."

She looked at him. He was serious. "Tell me about it."

"Nothing to tell. I just got scared, and I went to church, and that's it. Nothing else."

She laid a hand on her brother's shoulder. "I hope you've come to a turning point, Erik. You're a lot better person than you've ever allowed yourself to be. . . . What'll you do now?"

"Thought I'd go visit mom and dad for a few days. Dad'll be home for the weekend. Been a while since I've seen them."

"Use my phone to tell them you're coming."

He nodded and walked to the phone. But before he picked it up, he cocked his head and looked at her with a thoughtful expression. "I was right, wasn't I? Lover's quarrel."

"Oh, Erik!"

"The guy I met in the restaurant?"

Brooke didn't reply.

"I thought so. Something about him I liked right off. Not like your usual boyfriends. But why the quarrel?"

"If you must know, we didn't quarrel."

"Don't try to kid your younger brother! You were lashing out at me, but you were aiming at him," Erik said, picking up the phone. "I think my sister's finally fallen in love."

Chapter Eight

Hal Humphries was busy so he was brief. "Brooke, I called you in because I'm tired of waiting for firm word about the Baja trip. Is it on or off?"

"You got a preference?"

"Yeah. I like that Heartbeat angle, and you've got to come up with some terrific footage for the first segment. So guess who's going to Baja?"

"I can hardly wait," Brooke replied sarcastically.

"And Brooke, while you're getting the camera crew together and getting your tourist card and all, try to find time to squeeze in an interview for the 'Old Man.'"

"Oh! Who's he want interviewed?"

"Some doctor who's on that new board with you."

"I'm afraid to guess his name."

"No need to guess, Brooke. Doctor Gregory Cameron. Comes highly recommended."

"By whom?"

"By the 'Old Man.' Any higher recommendation possible?" The ND didn't expect Brooke to answer such an obvious question; he simply continued his orders. "And one thing more. The 'Old Man' wants that interview live."

"Live? What for? Videotape's far better!"

"Who knows what's gotten into the 'Old Man' lately? . . . Just do it." Hal Humphries turned to the papers on his desk to indicate there was no more time for discussion.

Brooke was the cool professional when she called Greg Cameron to set up an appointment for the following evening. Here was a golden opportunity to put him on the spot, and Brooke was determined to make the most of the opportunity. He'd squirm for the way he'd disrupted her life, and she'd do it live, on camera, before well over one hundred thousand viewers.

Her plan was simple: ask loaded questions that would expose the secret she was sure he was hiding—or at least make him look foolish. None of the latter would be easy, Brooke knew, for the doctor was suave and sophisticated and might be expecting a booby trap.

After the union makeup member arrived (the third in three weeks), and she fussed with him to get her facial colors just right, she went to her dressing room. She'd chosen a loden green, Evan Picone side-slit wool skirt with a her-ringbone tweed blazer. She wore a cream-colored silk shirt with a pair of Anne Klein low-heeled pumps.

Brooke took a deep breath and took the familiar walk from dressing room to studio. Even the newsroom Romeos whistled when Brooke walked onto the set. But Brooke paid no attention and walked across the room to greet Gregory Cameron, who wore a dark blue Louis Ross designer suit, white silk shirt, and navy blue tie. Dressed conservatively, his appearance would not distract the viewers' attention from his main objective—raising money for the North Bay Hospital wing. Greg had arrived a few minutes early and was engaged in a conversation with the "Six O'Clock Report" producer. Brooke sensed instantly that he knew a lot more about public relations and fund raising than she'd given him credit for.

"Good evening, Dr. Cameron," she said, extending her hand graciously. "Have you been briefed?"

"Not entirely," he said with a tinge of smile, which showed he appreciated her slender but well-formed figure. "I've been briefed on the interview, but I see something new has been added to the interviewer."

Brooke smiled at the compliment and explained that she'd do the regular news segment, then interview him right after the second commercial break.

He nodded and took a seat off to the side and behind camera one where he could watch both the monitor and the set at the same time. Brooke took her place and tried to still her rising pulse as she went over her interview strategy one more time.

"The floor is ready," she heard, which brought a professional smile to her lips. The floor manager's familiar seven-finger countdown began, and the crouching floor director swept his right hand silently toward camera one.

The standard introduction went off smoothly and the lead stories were aired. Brooke took care to read the TelePrompTer smoothly and easily, occasionally glancing at the papers in front of her to give the illusion she was not reading.

The first commercial came and went, and Brooke took up the news segment again, brightly including the weatherman and sportscaster in her casual, friendly remarks. It was a good show, more show biz than news, but good commercial television. When the second commercial break came, Brooke moved to a specially designed set a few feet to the right of the anchor desk. The doctor had already taken his place and was seated somewhat ill at ease before her in a deep upholstered chair.

"Comfortable?" she asked with a big smile.

"Not especially. But I want the public's support for that new hospital wing."

"As soon as this commercial has ended, you'll have your chance to show The City whose behind the new hospital wing."

He stiffened slightly, as though something had alerted him to her intentions. But the floor director called, "Stand by!" and Brooke held up a restraining hand to prevent him from speaking.

The red light silently winked on atop the camera. Brooke flashed her newsperson's smile and began talking. "We have with us tonight, live, in our studios, a distinguished physician and surgeon with a special interest in the new children's wing of North Bay Hospital.

"Dr. Gregory Cameron, welcome!"

"Thank you." He shifted slightly under the intense lights. His brown fingers fretted nervously with the cord, which led from his lapel microphone down the far side of his body away from the camera. He did not smile. In fact, he appeared moody, withdrawn, with a suggestion that he was going to be one of those horrible interviewees whose answers were limited to "Yes," "No," and "No comment"—a newsperson's nightmare. The thought startled Brooke as much as the apparent change in his demeanor.

"Doctor Cameron, tell us why the public should be interested in the new children's wing of your hospital."

"Excuse me, Miss Summers, it's not *my* hospital. It's the people's hospital, run by a board of directors responsible to the people.

"We all should support the construction of a new pediatric wing because it is our children who suffer disease, accidents, and birth defects. A compassionate city like San Francisco naturally wants to help alleviate any child's suffering, especially our own."

Brooke blinked in surprise. The withdrawn, reserved quality she thought she'd detected was gone. Greg Cameron was speaking quietly, but earnestly, with compassion in his voice.

"I have some color slides, Miss Summers, which your station has kindly consented to show. With your permission, I'd like to explain the stories behind them."

Again, Brooke blinked, but smiled and urged her guest to show the pictures. Yet an uneasy feeling began to seep into Brooke's mind. Not only had he quietly set up the stills before she came, but somehow the crew had forgotten—or neglected—to inform her. She began to feel a little foolish.

"This first one," Dr. Cameron said as the thirty-five millimeter slide appeared on the monitor, "shows why this hospital exists."

The little girl, perhaps five, stared gloomily from the monitor. She had a badly deformed left foot. But the doctor didn't linger on this dismal child.

"This next shot," he continued as the slide appeared on the monitor, "is what North Bay was able to do for her—because the people in our city care."

It was the same little girl, perhaps a year older, and smiling broadly. She stood upright on two good legs; her foot was straight and appeared normal. Even though the interview was still only about ninety seconds old, Brooke felt as if she was losing control. Greg Cameron was articulating the North Bay story so well, she knew it would be difficult to turn the focus of the dialogue on him. But she was still resolved to try. She asked another question while her mind frantically planned her subtle strategy.

"Doctor Cameron," Brooke said, smiling for the number two camera, which had dollied in on soundless rubber tires for a close-up, "a natural question would be: who pays for such remarkable hospital care?"

"Most of our patients' expenses are covered by insurance policies. But sometimes a child's family is uninsured for one reason or another, and they are unable to repay the medical debt.

That's where the caring people of San Francisco come in. They help give such children a new lease on life by direct, tax-deductible donations to the North Bay Hospital, which is a tax-exempt, nonprofit institution. Finances raised during this building project will be divided equally between construction costs, and the assistance of families who normally wouldn't be able to afford professional care for their children."

Greg Cameron was as ardent as an evangelist, Brooke suddenly realized. He was believable and highly persuasive. She felt herself softening.

But was his obvious emotion an act? Brooke pondered. How could the man who drove the fancy Italian sports car be the same doctor who cared for maimed and disformed children, who were sometimes even rejected by their own parents? If Greg Cameron wasn't acting, Brooke told herself, she'd made a serious mistake about him. But if he was, it was her duty—and her pleasure—to expose him in front of the viewing audience.

"Doctor Cameron, those were certainly heartwarming pictures and stories. Were they all your patients?"

"Some were; others were cared for by other doctors on staff at North Bay. But when it comes to sick or crippled children, Miss Summers, all children are everyone's children."

"I agree, Dr. Cameron," Brooke said as the producer whispered, "Two minutes," into her IFB unit. She froze for a second as she decided to ask Greg Cameron about himself. It was now or never.

"Doctor Cameron," Brooke began. "How did you happen to end up working with crippled children in San Francisco?"

Instantly, the dark eyes dropped; the handsome face sobered. The evangelistic zeal, which had animated his face slid away.

"Miss Summers, I'm sure there's nothing about my life which would be of interest to your viewers."

Until now Greg Cameron had controlled the direction of the interview. But Brooke could sense that he was perturbed enough that she could turn the tables on him. "Tell me how you got interested in medicine," she asked.

"There's nothing to tell . . . really," he added emphatically. "Now, Miss Summers . . ."

Brooke was annoyed. She knew Greg Cameron was hiding something; yet he was too noncommital for her to learn his secret. Well, maybe she could at least find out what kind of man he really was!

"You'd do anything for those children, wouldn't you, Dr. Cameron?"

"I do what I can."

"Even outside the San Francisco area, in places like Mexico's Baja peninsula?

"I've been to Baja, among other places," he admitted carefully.

"Would you go again? I mean, if you could help some sick or crippled children there?"

He was very alert now. "Of course, Miss Summers," he said softly, guardedly, his tensions apparent to her but not to the television cameras.

"Would you fly to Baja this weekend with some other doctors and nurses to donate your services to an orphanage there?"

"Ordinarily, Miss Summers, I'd be glad to help out. But I already have plans. . . ."

"Plans more important than orphans?" She hated herself the moment the words were out of her mouth, but she'd determined to make the most of her opportunity.

He was trapped, and they both knew it. But he was gracious and charming. He picked up her barb and turned it neatly aside. "Miss Summers, nothing is more important than helping those children. I'm delighted you asked me. Of course I'll cancel my other plans and accept. You are going, too, aren't you, Miss Summers?"

Deftly, he had turned his own trap into one for her. Out of the corner of her eye she saw camera three dolly in silently for a close-up of her face. She managed a full smile.

"Of course, Dr. Cameron. A film crew is also standing by, so we'll have a special feature for our audience next week. Thank you, for being our guest. We'll be right back with the rest of the 'Six O'Clock Report' right after this word."

The red camera light winked out, and the monitor showed a commercial. Brooke stood quickly, but Dr. Cameron was faster.

"You're a very clever woman, Miss Summers," he said with quiet control so the rest of the crew couldn't hear. "I only hope you weren't too clever. Good night!"

He spun abruptly and walked briskly off the set. Brooke wanted to call after him, but she knew the crew was too close. And often, the cameras were on her so the producer and other news personnel in the control room could see her even when the signal wasn't going out on the air. Brooke managed a pleasant smile and called, "We're leaving from the executive terminal tomorrow morning at 5:30."

He didn't stop or turn around. Brooke watched him push the door open and turn into the hallway toward the elevator. She felt her stomach churn and her blood race. She was going to Baja again, and half of San Francisco knew it!

Chapter Nine

Brooke's alarm rang three short hours after she had exhaustedly crawled into bed. She took a quick shower, hurriedly applied a new coat of makeup, and threw some things in a small suitcase, arriving at the airport right on schedule: 5: 30 A.M. Everyone else, including Greg Cameron, was ready and waiting.

Introductions were brief, and the three light planes soon followed each other down the strip and lifted into the September morning air. They turned over the bay, and the mini-convoy headed south along the rugged California coast. The first leg of the long, nine-hour flight had begun without any complications. Brooke hoped the smooth departure was indicative of the entire trip.

Scotty led the caravan in a low-winged model, which had a name Brooke forgot as soon as he told her. The second plane was a black-and-red one almost identical to Scotty's. Brooke remembered the third plane's name: a high-winged blue and white Cessna. Her father had once owned one like it. All three were light, single-engine aircraft.

Brooke had chosen to fly with Scotty in the lead plane, and was seated to his right. She had offers to ride in both of the other planes, but had graciously refused when she learned that one pilot, Dan Roberts, was a dentist, and the other, Carla Simpson, was a nurse (weekend pilots—as they were known in the newsroom). She had covered enough private plane crashes to know she would feel more secure with Scotty, a rated Marine helicopter pilot who'd flown crop dusting and fixed-wing aircraft before and after his military service.

Pepe Martinez, the bilingual Channel Three cameraman, and Jeff Shaker, the soundman, were behind Scotty and Brooke. Every other space was crammed with equipment, baggage, and ready-to-eat food. Brooke wasn't too thrilled about Jeff's presence since the divorced bachelor often tried to corner her, but he was a good technician.

Brooke liked to watch Scotty when he was behind the controls; it often seemed like he was a part of the aircraft. His hand was on the throttle, gently, seeming to communicate with the plane's twenty-three hundred pounds of aluminum. The speedometer indicated they were cruising at about one hundred and twenty knots.

The foursome, veterans of many flights together, tired of small talk and settled down to silence, hearing the drone of the engine. Brooke wondered how Greg Cameron was getting along with his fellow passengers. He had chosen to fly with Dan Roberts, D.D.S., active Christian layman whose interest in helping others had often taken him to Baja. Riding with him was another dentist, Dr. Sid Koch, and a pediatrician, Dr. George Ross.

Brooke wondered if Carla Simpson, the third pilot, was of Latin descent. Probably, Brooke decided, because Carla spoke Spanish as did Pepe. Carla's passengers included a general practitioner, Dr. Pete Callos, and a layman, Art Demsey, who was a handyman with a special interest in missions.

Brooke shifted her position and took a long look at the landscape below her. The jagged coastal mountains of western California had given way to a sea of freeways and houses stretching in every direction. Smog limited visibility to about eight miles, and Brooke guessed they were flying over the Los Angeles basin.

She soon tired of watching L.A.'s seemingly endless congestion and leaned back in her seat, closing her eyes.

She couldn't keep her mind off the man in the other plane. She had seen a Greg Cameron who could be a charming gentleman, and one who could upset her to the boiling point. She had seen a man who had displayed physical affection for her; and a man who remained cold and aloof. What kind of a Greg Cameron would she see this weekend? Certainly, they'd have to be together some of the time.

Scotty's voice broke her reverie. "Tijuana Airport coming up. We've got to stop here as the first port of entry. We'll have customs and immigration to clear, then we'll be on our way to Guerrero Negro. After that, it can get hairy."

"Hairy?" Brooke asked, concern showing in her voice.

"Nothing to worry about, Brooke! But Baja has some of the trickiest winds in the world. Sometimes that can make things interesting!"

Brooke's watch read 9: 45 as Scotty rolled the plane to a stop. Brooke noted that they had been in the air close to four hours, and realized they had still only come halfway. The other two planes followed close behind in the landing pattern. Soon the three aircraft taxied over to the terminal to refuel.

The dentist walked over to Brooke and Scotty with a look of greeting on his face. He was a short, graying man in his early forties. He wore bifocals with metal frames and a casual shirt. Brooke's eyes automatically went beyond Dr. Roberts to Greg. He was talking to Carla Simpson as they watched the Mexican officials make routine checks of their planes.

"Miss Summers . . ."

"Brooke." She smiled at the dentist.

"Brooke," he nodded. "I'm Dan. Sorry we didn't get better acquainted back there before we took off. I've heard some interesting things about you, however."

Brooke felt her interest go up. Greg had been talking about her! "Oh?" she said, trying to be casual.

"Yes, indeed. I think I've learned more about you in this flight than if I'd talked to you personally. You're really quite a go-getter."

Brooke tried to control her disappointment.

So that's how Greg described her? "And what did you find out about the good doctor flying with you?" she asked.

The dentist shook his head. "Not much, now that you mention it. I came over to say that we'll have an opportunity to attend a church service tomorrow. Might be an experience if this is your first time south of the border."

"I've been down before," Brooke said. "I had sworn I'd never come again."

Scotty broke in. "I told her there's nothing to be concerned about. Thousands of Americans visit Mexico all the time."

"Be careful of the meat if we get invited to someone's home after church," Dan Roberts warned. "Usually, there's not a problem, but sometimes the meat contains a virulent virus that doesn't die in the cooking. It is not only hard on you at the time, but some of those nasty little bugs stay in your system."

"Oh, thanks!" Brooke groaned. "That's all I needed!"

The dentist sensed things would have been better if he had kept his advice to himself. "Guess I shouldn't have said that, but most people don't know about the beef. I wanted to make sure you didn't get caught on this trip."

She waved the thought aside. "What kind of church will we attend?"

"A little evangelistic Protestant one near Guerrero Negro. Some evangelical pastors down there are doing a terrific job, and this church shows the results of one man's faith and hard work. . . . Well, if I'm going to stretch my legs before we take off again, I better get going. Talk to you later."

Scotty sensed Brooke's feelings. "Don't worry, Brooke. This is going to be an unforgettable trip."

"That's what I'm afraid of." She tried to make it sound like a joke.

She looked at the tiny little aircraft in which she'd flown into another country and another world. The uneasy feeling she had had about the trip, returned stronger than ever.

It was still with her when the air caravan took off toward Guerrero Negro, some five hundred miles below the border.

Once they were up in the air and Scotty seemed to relax from the concentration of the takeoff, Brooke pointed to the controls before them. "Somehow I'd feel a lot better if I understood some of what was going on. I never flew enough with dad to learn anything."

"There's nothing to it, really. I'll show you."

From his position on her left, Scotty pointed out the fixed-wing's features. The wheellike control was called the yoke. It was a glistening black object, which Scotty could pull back or shove forward. It controlled the pitch attitude, he said, the up-or-down motion, and banking left or right.

"I pull back on the yoke, and the nose comes up on the aircraft. You must have noticed that on takeoff."

"Yes," Brooke said pensively. "But what I'd really like to know, Scotty, is what kind of problems we could run into flying in such remote areas. You know the old adage: 'Forewarned is forearmed.' "

"Well, our biggest problem is likely to be bad fuel.

"In the old days, we used to strain everything through a chamois down here. Takes out water—or dirt."

"I don't understand, Scotty."

"When a little water gets in aviation gasoline, which sometimes happens in these remote areas, the water goes to the bottom of the fuel tank because the gas is lighter. Soon as the good gas in the fuel line is used up—which is usually right after you take off, the water gets sucked up. And down she goes!" He made a sharp downward slant with his extended palm.

"The plane?"

"Yes, but don't worry. I'm going to have the attendant use a chamois when we refuel deep in Baja. That not only takes care of the water problem, but if there's any dirt or contaminants in the fuel, it'll be strained out."

"What would happen if that wasn't done?"

"The contaminants destroy the fuel pump or plug the filter in the carburetor. Maybe the fuel wouldn't ignite properly and down we'd go again!"

"Scotty, you're scaring me!"

"Didn't mean to," he said with a smile. "But you asked. I can't rightly ask for 'no incidents,' because there's not a pilot alive who doesn't have some scary moments if he flies long enough. But safety is something I do ask the Lord to give us."

"You're not making me feel a whole lot better, Scotty."

"Relax, Brooke! I'm not going to do anything foolish! And I never let my faith overrule my common sense and God's physical laws. Well, here's Guerrero ahead of us. Make sure your seat belt's snug."

As they made their approach Scotty banked the little plane so his passengers could see the layout of the land around the small village.

"Biggest airport in these parts. Dirt landing strip goes uphill, so when you're standing down there watching a plane land, it goes up a little rise, then out of sight beyond the hill. Of course, the dust from the prop helps hide the aircraft, too. No tower, just a wind sock. See it? No wind today."

Pepe and Jeff were more interested in the great body of water a short distance from the airport.

"Scammon Lagoon," Scotty told them without taking his eyes off his landing check of the instruments. "That's where the gray whales come to play on the surface during certain seasons.

"And that pretty-looking necklace of sand you see around the lagoon and stretching inland so far," Scotty added, "is the Vizcaino Desert."

Pepe broke his habitual silence. *"Desierto de Vizcaino,"* he said with a touch of awe. "I have heard of that place."

"What've you heard, Pepe?" Brooke asked, looking over her shoulder at the cameraman.

He shrugged, his thin black moustache curving up as he forced a wan smile. "Nothing to be concerned about."

Brooke wasn't satisfied with his answer, but the plane's nose was pointed down and ground was coming up fast before them. The landing strip stretched out dead ahead of the spinning prop.

"Maybe we'll get to have some sea turtle," Jeff said. "I hear it's a real delicacy around here."

Brooke wasn't listening. She was watching as Scotty swung the nose slightly to the right, correcting the approach just a trifle. Whatever it was that had concerned her about the flight was almost over. She held her breath as the little plane settled, touched, and rolled.

"Thank God!" she said softly to herself. "We're down safely."

Brooke didn't see anyone standing on the airstrip to greet them. She knew there were no telephones within several hundred miles, and letters, arriving by either boat or plane often took weeks. Consequently, no one knew that they were coming.

The other two planes followed Scotty down and created a cloud of dust, which several minutes later, was still slowly drifting over the barren hills to the east. They had landed during the heat of the day, and the lack of breeze made the 100° afternoon feel more like 120. Brooke could remember days in Bakersfield when it felt as unpleasant as this, but never did she remember feeling so hot in San Francisco.

As she watched the people emerge from the other two planes, her thoughts turned to why they had flown one thousand miles into one of the world's most desolate areas. She and the KBRG camera crew had come south to put a story of some unfortunate little orphans on film: a story, Brooke knew, that would tug at the emotions of San Francisco viewers for a few moments, and then be totally forgotten five minutes later. But those few minutes of "emotional pull" could potentially mean higher ratings for her program.

Carla, Dan, Sid, George, Pete, and Art, on the

other hand, had flown to south Baja because of their Christian love for the people. All of these highly trained professionals were giving up their holiday weekend so the local people could have a little bit better life. Brooke felt a touch of shame as she compared her motivations to theirs.

Only twenty minutes after they had landed, a dusty old pickup truck bounced toward them. Scotty looked up, shading his eyes against the sun. "Looks as if we're going to have company, folks."

The dentist stopped unloading some of his equipment and glanced at the swirling dust that marked the truck's progress. "That'll be Alfonso Morales. He's the local evangelical pastor I told you about."

Pepe smiled. "I heard that when you *gringos* came down here with your Protestant religion, it was illegal to say the pastor was a missionary, so they said they were teachers. Now," he shrugged, "I have heard there are many of these churches and everyone gets along."

"That's because we *gringos* planted evangelical churches and helped train your local pastors, like Alfonso, so they could take over." Dan Roberts, the dentist, said. "Get ready for a Baja California Sur greeting!"

As Roberts had predicted Alfonso Morales joyously hugged the members of the medical team who'd been to Baja before, and graciously welcomed the newcomers like Brooke.

"I haf been praying you would come," the local pastor said with a great smile and a wide-open, sweeping motion of his powerful, bare arms. He was a stocky man whose Indian features reflected the Mexicans' Indian heritage.

"I haf believed you were coming, so everything is ready. A place for the senora and senorita to sleep away from the scorpions. Another place—"

"Scorpions?" Brooke exclaimed, instantly regretting it.

The pastor smiled broadly. "Haf no fear, senorita. I haf invited the scorpions to leave, and I believe they have done that!"

Brooke tried to return the pastor's smile and to ease the minds of the others who were reassuring her. But suddenly she had an overpowering awareness that she was in a foreign country, in a different culture, among those who spoke a tongue unfamiliar to her. Her only means of returning was the tiny single-engine aircraft.

Beyond the pastor, Brooke caught a glimpse of Greg Cameron. He had taken a break from unloading the bags, food, and water from the planes, and was watching her. For a moment, their eyes met and held. His were slitted, perhaps against the sun, but more likely, Brooke felt, because he was absorbed by his own thoughts. What was it that made him keep everything to himself? she wondered.

"Señores, señora, señorita," Alfonso called, sliding the last bag into the pickup. "You will haf to ride on the back with the dust, except for the ladies. They will ride in the cab with me. We will offer you a shower, a chance to change your clothing, and then—if you wish—we will haf time to fly to the orphanage before the sun she is down."

"I thought the orphanage was here?" Brooke asked, trying to conceal her disappointment.

"Ah, no, *señorita!* It is a half-hour flight. But there is time to go and return before sundown. Perhaps you can get some peektures, no? Then tomorrow we shall have the worship service and take more peektures. *Es verdad,* Dr. Roberts?"

Brooke turned to Scotty. He was looking at his aircraft. "I'd better make sure they use a chamois when they refuel my plane. It's such a short flight, but I don't want to take any chances. You go on ahead. I'll skip the shower."

Couldn't we just wait until tomorrow? Brooke wanted to protest. Instead, she said, "Who's going on this hop?"

Scotty mused, "Well, let's see. You've got to have a pilot, so I'll go. We'll need Pepe and his camera, of course, but we can do a voice-over later, and so we won't need Jeff and his sound equipment. We'll need you, Brooke, to be on camera with a doctor. That's four; all this plane will carry."

"What about you, Pastor Morales?" Brooke asked.

"Ah, senorita! They haf seen my face many times! They would rather see you and the camera, I am sure; and the infirm ones—should there be any—would like to see the doctor. Since *Hermano* Scotty has been there before, he knows everyone, and they will welcome heem! Now, which of you doctors will volunteer to see *los niños?*"

"I'll go," Greg Cameron said quietly.

Technically, Brooke was in charge of the news crew; she had no control over Scotty and the doctors. But she didn't want to be cooped up in a little airplane with the two men in her life.

"Maybe," she suggested, trying to keep her own insecurities from showing, "I should stay behind and let the nurse or another doctor go with Scotty and Dr. Cameron."

Greg looked at her with an expressionless face. "Are you afraid, Brooke?"

It was a challenge, and Brooke recognized it as something like a childish dare. But she was not going to lose her chance at a good feature story just because she was uneasy.

"Of course not!"

"Good!" Greg said, his face not changing expression. "Then let's get cleaned up and be on our way to that orphanage!"

Brooke sighed. She had always tried to control her destiny. But somehow things seemed to be slipping from her, and she didn't like that at all. Not at all!

Chapter Ten

The foursome flying on to Soledad had
freshened up quickly, and were in the air in less
than an hour. Pepe and Greg sat silently in the
back, while Scotty filled them in on what to expect once they arrived. Suddenly, Scotty
stopped his description in midsentence.
Brooke knew why an instant later. Her heart
seemed to pause as she listened to the sputter-
ing of the engine.

Scotty's fingers moved instantly, automatically, but the engine sputtered again, coughed,
and died. A terrible stillness suddenly filled
the little cabin. All was quiet, except for the
eerie sound of the wind blowing against the
wings.

Scotty said softly, "Got a little problem,
folks." His voice was matter of fact, as if what
had happened was no big deal. "Just sit tight

and everything'll be OK."

Brooke watched in horrified fascination as the pilot's coaxing fingers failed to restart the engine. Then she stole a quick glance out the window. The brown earth seemed to be rushing up to meet them with surprising speed. They had been flying at low altitude, having started their descent toward Soledad, which was still out of sight beyond a range of low mountains. Brooke was trying to forget the crashes she'd covered in her news career when Greg's voice came from the backseat. "Can I help, Scotty?"

"No, thanks." Scotty's voice was amazingly calm. "I've done these dead-stick landings before. If we can just stay out of that Vizcaino Desert and coax her onto that flat, brushy shelf—"

He didn't finish. Brooke saw a deep canyon at the far end of the proposed landing site, and thought she heard Pepe muttering something in Spanish—a prayer, probably. Then the ground was below them.

"Lord!" Scotty's voice was only slightly animated as the plane fought to go in nose first, "I'd appreciate a little help to keep her from nosing over!"

The little plane hit hard, lurched into the air, snapping Brooke's head about, and then they were down evenly, rolling fast and hard. She saw Scotty fighting to keep the nose up and the direction straight. He applied pressure on the brakes firmly but not enough to tip forward.

Then they stopped, and Scotty breathed a big sigh of relief.

Brooke was trembling uncontrollably when she stepped out onto the low, brushlike growth, which dotted the sandy earth. Pepe leaped down behind her and crossed himself. Greg followed Scotty out, and both men hurried to her.

"You all right?" They asked it together.

Brooke tried to stop shaking, but the nervous pulsations continued. Each man moved to her side, Scotty to the right, Greg to the left. They held her while she fought for control of her emotions.

"I'm sorry, Brooke," Scotty said. "She was flying along just beautifully until all of a sudden . . ."

Greg interrupted, "I thought you had the fuel run through a chamois back there?"

"I did, but sometimes a little sediment slips by, anyway. Hey! We're getting a little wind out here. Not steady, either. See how it's eddying instead of blowing from one direction?"

Brooke looked at her clothes, which were flapping about, first one way and then another. It didn't mean anything to her. She glanced around and for the first time, took a good look at the surrounding landscape. It was desolate-looking country, totally devoid of houses, animals, or people. There was only low brush and the rough-appearing terrain. It reminded Brooke of some B movies she had seen as a kid that were supposedly set on the planet Mars. "How do we get out of here?" she asked with a shudder.

"No problem," Scotty assured her. "I suspect we've got a little sediment in the carburetor. If that's all it is, we'll be on our way in no time."

Brooke glanced apprehensively at their situation. They'd landed in a sagebrush field and were facing slightly uphill. Brooke instinctively knew Scotty had chosen that to help stop his roll. Still, it looked too short for a successful takeoff.

Greg was thinking the same thing. "You sure we can make it safely, Scotty?"

"No problem! I'll turn her around after taxiing to the top of this little rise, and then we'll gain a little speed going downhill."

Pepe whispered, looking at the proposed takeoff route, "But the hill! That hill at the end is all rocks, boulders! And beyond it—a canyon!"

Scotty nodded. "We'll just have to pull her nose up sharply and jump over those boulders. I'll pull up the landing gear fast to cut down on the drag. Then we'll head out over the canyon and climb out."

Scotty paused a moment before he articulated his next thought. "I just wish this strange Baja wind wouldn't keep changing its mind about which way it's going to blow."

"What happens if the wind doesn't cooperate," Brooke forced herself to ask. "Or you don't get up sufficient flying speed by the time we reach those boulders and the canyon?"

"Once I heard about a plane that didn't have flying speed when it went off a plateau over a canyon like that. By sticking her nose down sharply, the pilot was able to pick up enough speed to fly it out."

Brooke was incredulous. "Are you suggesting that we are going to dive into that canyon?"

Scotty nodded somberly. "We'll lighten the load as much as possible. Have to leave one of you here for a while, along with the camera equipment. I'll fly back to Guerrero Negro, change to Carla's lighter plane, and come back for that person. You, maybe, Pepe?"

The *latino* nodded vigorously, so Scotty turned to Greg and Brooke. "I'll take you two off with me. Or you're welcome to stay here until you've had a chance to watch me demonstrate my theory."

"I trust your judgment, Scotty," Greg responded. "I'll go out with you when you're ready."

Brooke hesitated, then said, "Me, too, Scotty."

The pilot smiled and turned to work on his engine.

Brooke had calmed down considerably, but she still had a strong feeling of anxiety over their predicament. She was in no mood to talk with either Greg or Scotty, so she decided to take a stroll and personally inspect their emergency airstrip. Her eyes kept a careful lookout for sidewinders and scorpions as she walked the entire length of the small plateau. She estimated the biggest boulders to be about as high as a garage, and saw that they were spread out over the entire width of the makeshift runway. She shuddered at the thought of what those giant rocks would do to a small airplane.

Brooke found a path through the huge rocks and walked another twenty yards to the canyon edge. It was much deeper than it looked from the air. She tossed a small rock over the side and waited for what seemed like an eternity until it bounced in the dry riverbed far below.

"Brooke." She heard someone call and she turned to see Greg walking toward her. "Your pilot friend has found the trouble. It's the car buretor, as he suspected. He says it'll be no trouble to fix, and we can go on to the orphanage."

"Go on? But he said we'd go back to Guerrero Negro."

"He's sure there's not going to be any further trouble."

"He didn't expect any trouble in the first place," Brooke exclaimed.

"He's the pilot, and we have to trust his judgment."

Brooke turned to look at Scotty as he stepped back from the plane and wiped his hands. Pepe was standing slightly beyond the right wing, his hands moving restlessly from pocket to pocket as though he'd lost something, or wasn't aware he was doing anything. Brooke turned back to Greg and decided to volunteer something that had been on her mind.

"You know, I've been doing a lot of thinking today," she said. "And I've learned something about myself."

"What's that, Brooke?"

"When I'm at the studio in San Francisco, I almost always feel like I'm in control of every situation. Sure, there are deadlines and sometimes there is intense pressure. But I usually feel like I'm on top of things."

She paused and looked at the rocky walls on the other side of the canyon. "Today, out here, I feel like there is not one thing I can do about what happens. And I don't like that."

"I know how you feel, Brooke. When I'm in the operating room, on familiar territory, I feel secure . . . that's the point here: Scotty's a mighty fine pilot. If that engine turns over and runs, as he believes it will, we have to believe he can take off safely."

Brooke suppressed a shudder. Greg saw the tremor and reached out to hold her. Then he hesitated until she met his eyes. They were a deep brown, but soft with concern. She moved a trifle so her shoulder touched his arm. His arm went around her quickly and wrapped her warmly and securely.

Brooke took one last quick look in Scotty's direction before she closed her eyes and drowned her fears in Greg's warm embrace. Glad that a boulder blocked Scotty's view, she knew how hurt he would be if he sensed that Greg Cameron represented competition.

Brooke was still so confused about her feelings toward Greg Cameron, she knew she would never be able to explain to Scotty something she didn't understand herself. But right now she didn't care. Somehow she felt safe in the doctor's strong arms.

Everything was ready. Pepe would stay on the ground and shoot footage of the takeoff. It had been his idea, but Brooke suspected it was more than a willingness to be working.

Scotty once again expressed his confidence that there would be no problem. The plan was to take both Brooke and Greg to the orphanage so the doctor could see if anyone needed his services. In the meantime, Brooke could be lining up some shots for tomorrow.

Hesitantly Brooke took her place beside Scotty and fastened her shoulder harness snugly as Greg got in behind them. Then Scotty revved the engine in neutral and put his feet on the brakes until the little aircraft seemed about to shake apart. Satisfied that the engine wasn't missing, Scotty eased off on the throttle and let the engine idle.

"Folks, we need sixty-five knots for flying speed. Say a prayer because here we go."

Scotty taxied up to the far end of the rough, uneven ground and whipped the little plane around in a cloud of dust. He wasted no time once they were pointed in the right direction and applied the throttle. His other hand gripped the yoke as they gathered speed downhill. The wings rocked as they bounced. The plane was jumping so much on the uneven ground that Brooke was sure they were going to ground-loop. She bit her lip and braced herself, straining to see the pile of boulders directly in their path.

The little engine was winding up, screaming with the demands Scotty was making. But the wheels were still thumping omniously on the ground, and Brooke thought she could hear the short brush catching against the under-carriage— or perhaps even the delicate fabric of the wings. Brooke watched in fascinated horror as the ground speed indicator struggled upward on the gauge in front of Scotty. The moment it touched sixty-five, he pulled the yoke back.

The aircraft lifted and the rumbling stopped. They were airborne. But Brooke was convinced they were still going to be smashed to bits by the giant rocks.

"OK, Lord!" Scotty's voice was still calm, but there was a hint of urgency the moment the wheels cleared the ground. "Wheels . . . up! And don't let us touch down again!"

During the next few seconds, Brooke felt the landing gear thunk into the housing and the plane's speed increased noticeably. Still, they weren't but more than eight or ten feet off the ground.

Brooke pressed back against the seat, trying to avoid the onrushing boulders. Suddenly, with a sickening wrench, Scotty applied power and yanked back hard on the yoke. The little airplane lurched upward, staggered drunkenly, and seemed to lose speed.

Brooke saw the boulders flash beneath the silver whirl of the propeller, and they were instantly lost to sight. The last few feet of earth slipped beneath the engine, which labored and screamed under Scotty's demand, and the canyon floated awesomely before them.

For a moment, it looked as though they were going to make it. Then Brooke felt a powerful gust of wind smack the little plane like a giant hand. It tipped sideways. Scotty tried to compensate. But he had been caught off guard. It was too late.

The aircraft sank sickeningly, straight down. The nose was still trying to climb up, but the entire plane was falling like a dropped stone.

Brooke tried not to scream. She leaned far back in the seat, feeling the shoulder harness cut into her right and left shoulder blades. Then Scotty shoved the yoke hard forward, forcing the nose sharply down toward the canyon floor.

"Oh, no!" Brooke hardly recognized her own voice. She sensed that Scotty was taking a desperate gamble in order to gain flying speed. Even though she didn't understand the aerodynamics of the move, she knew he wasn't deliberately trying to crash nose first into the deep canyon.

Brooke saw the rocky canyon floor rushing up with horrible speed toward the spinning propeller, which was biting futilely into the air in a last desperate effort to prevent a flaming crash.

Chapter Eleven

Brooke couldn't take her eyes off the fast approaching canyon floor. The throttle was wide open as they sped to what Brooke felt would be certain death in a blazing inferno. She was aware her mouth was open, but wasn't sure if she was screaming or not. All she could hear was the roar of the valiant little engine as Scotty pushed it to the limit.

Then Brooke faintly heard Scotty's voice above the motor's din. "Lord!" The pragmatism was still there, but so was an urgency. "I need a little help . . . right . . . *now!*"

Out of the corner of her eye, Brooke saw Scotty's hands suddenly pull back on the yoke. She felt a surge of power as the plane fought to stop its plunge and reverse direction.

Scotty's hands turned white and the muscles in his shoulders knotted as he tried to lean back. Just when it seemed like they could drop no further, the engine changed sounds. The engine cowling, which had seemed to be vibrating so hard it would fly off, settled down as the propeller bit solidly into the air. In a moment, the plane's course ran parallel to the canyon bottom, and then slowly, laboriously, they began to gain altitude.

Scotty laughed. It was a little ragged. "Oh, thank you, Father! Up, now! . . . Up!"

Slowly, obediently, the nose continued to lift and the canyon floor retreated below them.

"Brooke, Greg!" Scotty's voice was jubilant. "That guy I read about—the one who said you could stick a plane's nose down in a power dive and gain flying speed over a canyon—he was sure right."

Greg's voice came from the backseat, calm and low. "Either that, or you sure say a mighty powerful prayer!"

"Maybe both!" Scotty exclaimed. Now that the danger was over and the plane was climbing smoothly out of the canyon, the adrenaline pouring through his bloodstream was forcing some of the pragmatism out of his voice.

Brooke's voice came out high and thin, startling her. "Scotty, I hope I don't ever have to fly in one of these things again. But if I do, I'd want you at the controls."

He thanked her and banked into the sky, circling to wag reassuring wings at Pepe, the cameraman. He still had the shoulder-mounted camera to his eye, following the little plane's rise above the canyon walls and up into the sky.

Scotty pointed. "Look at that, would you! What a cameraman! What footage he must have shot!

If he kept that camera on us from takeoff to now, Brooke, you've already got one of the greatest live-action sequences any television personality could ask for!"

Brooke nodded but didn't answer. In that stomach-wrenching plunge over the canyon, when she was sure death was seconds away, Brooke had sensed something—no, more than sensed—she had known something for a certainty.

Brooke leaned back against the seat and closed her eyes. She knew God had answered Scotty's prayers for safety. The God she had put out of her life for so long was real, and he was still there waiting for Brooke to trust in him again. She thought of the spiritual commitments she had made at Bible camp in junior and senior high school, but had since broken.

In college she had determined that she wanted a glamorous life in broadcasting. When success started to come, she had quietly packed her Bible away. She wondered what kind of shape she would be in if this had been the day she entered eternity.

Brooke opened her eyes and was aware that Scotty and Greg were still engaged in loud conversation as they shared the euphoria of their successful takeoff. They had left her alone, apparently interpreting her silence for relief after their escape from death.

The little plane slanted downward again, gently, and Brooke saw a village and crude landing strip carved out of the desert.

"That's the town of Soledad," Scotty explained. "See all that agriculture? Irrigation has allowed them to grow fig trees, melons, and other fruits in the middle of this desolate desert. More than a thousand kids are in that orphanage over to your right. Their parents were killed by a hurricane, which also washed out a dirt dam and literally drowned several communities."

The plane landed and bounced along the unpaved runway, trailing dust. When the single-engine aircraft had come to a complete stop, Brooke unbuckled her shoulder harness and stepped out onto the wing and down to the desert floor. People were already running toward them.

Scotty pointed out the sights when he and Greg were also on the ground. "There's one house of cardboard with a frond roof and some beat-up wood to hold it all together. But most of the houses, as you can see, have asbestos shingles over concrete block buildings. They're small but clean, with kerosene lamps and running water. That's the local church Pastor Morales built for the *maestros*, the disciples. We helped him a little, but mostly local believers, *hermanos* (which means brothers), did the work."

The church was made of red brick. It was small, perhaps seating a hundred people. A small frond building, almost like a fence, housed the gasoline compressor, Scotty explained, so the church had electric lights. The orphanage also had electricity provided by another compressor, which was only run for a couple of hours after dark.

The *hermanos* and *hermanas*, as Scotty called them, surrounded the newcomers, greeting Scotty in Spanish and grinning happily as they

welcomed the others. Brooke was surprised to
see how old the women looked, even though
they were probably under thirty because most
held infants on their hips. Many were missing
front teeth.

Brooke acknowledged introductions with a
smile and what few Spanish salutations she
could remember. Doctor Greg Cameron, on the
other hand, responded in flawless Spanish.
Once the greetings were over, most of the com-
munity led them the short distance from the
airstrip to the orphanage. Children peeked
shyly from an outside drinking fountain, which
Brooke hadn't expected to see, and from behind
doors. She smiled, and they smiled back. The
trio was led inside and presented to the *ma-
trona,* a heavy woman, who wore the same simple clothes as the townspeople. She hugged the
young American girl exuberantly, almost
smothering Brooke in her ample bosom.

"They certainly are friendly enough!" Brooke
said to Scotty and Greg. "Wish I could understand what everyone is saying, but my high
school Spanish is too rusty."

Scotty chuckled. "They're saying we are welcome in their town, and that we must have dinner with them. I speak only enough of the language to get by, but I've told them *el doctor* will
want to wash his hands and examine the children, and you, Brooke, will want to see *los niños.*
I have to get back to Guerrero Negro and rescue
Pepe before darkness falls. You two will be on
your own, but that'll be no problem, seeing as
Greg speaks the language. And Hernando, the *el
jefe,* or chief around here, will take care of you."

Hernando, a big man whose graying hairs

were rapidly claiming his heavy head of coal black hair, was almost in tears when he hugged Scotty good-bye.

The *jefe* and *madroña* accompanied the two *norteamericanos* from room to room where the children slept in homemade bunks. Brooke noticed calendars on the walls with pictures of flowers and animals.

As they left another neat, small room, which was home to its young occupants, Brooke admitted, "They're starting to get to me. Emotionally, I mean."

"Is that bad, Brooke?"

"I don't know. Theoretically, a professional shouldn't let the heart get mixed up with business. But those darling children!"

Greg smiled at her. "It is necessary not only to have a heart, but to allow it to function as God intended."

The reference to God made Brooke's eyes widen. Brooke had always wondered why she had seen Greg Cameron in church, especially since his life-style and conversation didn't indicate any kind of belief. For the first time, she wondered if he had once possessed a vibrant faith, just as she had.

The Mexican administrator held open a large, double door and said something in Spanish. Greg answered him, then turned to Brooke again.

"He has some sick children in here and thinks it's best if I go in alone. Would you like one of the women to show you around? Maybe line up some footage?"

Brooke thought for a moment. "No, if you don't mind, I'd like to go in with you."

He studied her thoughtfully, then shrugged. "Whatever you say."

Greg told Hernando that Brooke would like to join him on his rounds, so the *jefe* opened the door to the hospital section of the orphanage.

"Buenos dias, muchachos," Greg said, immediately moving forward to the first two boys who lay quietly on beds nearest the door. Brooke didn't catch the rest of the words as Greg continued in his fluent Spanish, but she guessed he had introduced himself. Hernando said a few more words to all of the children and left the two of them on their own.

The first boy was about eight, Brooke guessed. He was shy and kept his chin down. The other boy was perhaps ten, and more bold. He met the friendly gaze of the "gringo" doctor with confidence, so Greg switched his questions to him. Soon the younger boy's head came up, and he interjected a short remark, which made Greg smile. He pointed shyly to his right hip.

"He says a scorpion bit him on his bare leg. But he is afraid to show me in front of the *señorita*. I suspect the sting is higher than the leg."

Brooke nodded. "Modesty must be honored. I'll leave so you can get on with the examination."

"Not yet," Greg said. "I'd like you to stay while I talk to the others, including that pretty, brown-eyed girl in the end bed."

The doctor moved on, chatting with each child in the next several beds. Brooke couldn't understand much of what he said, but she did notice how at ease he was with the children. He spoke softly, reassuringly, making them smile or even laugh. Finally, Greg Cameron arrived at the little girl's bedside. Brooke noticed that she did not smile, and her face showed pain. A faint, unpleasant odor permeated the air.

Greg turned soberly to Brooke. "She says a lamp fell and hot kerosene splattered on her foot. I'm going to wash up again and have a look at it. But my nose already tells me what I'm going to find under that bandage. Would you mind staying with her until I get back?"

"Of course not. But what'll I say?"

"Say it with your eyes. Show her the same love you've been giving to those other kids."

Brooke was touched by Greg's compliment. She also wondered if her eyes had told Greg anything about her feelings for him. She hoped he didn't realize how much he was stirring her emotions.

Brooke smiled at the little girl, spoke reassuringly, and tentatively reached out a hand. The girl pulled back, uncertainly, and then let Brooke gently stroke her long, dark hair. She was still doing that when Greg spoke from behind her.

"You're very gentle with children, Brooke."

"No more so than you, *señor doctor*. You've completely won the heart of every kid in here."

Greg grinned wryly. "I hope they're still grinning when I get through examining them. But I can tell right now this little girl probably needs more medical attention than I can give her here. I don't think you'll want to see the wound."

"If she has to suffer with the pain, I guess I can stand to see her injury."

"OK, but I suggest you get a tight rein on your emotions. I don't want her to see your reaction."

Brooke stiffened, fought a feeling of fright, and turned to the little girl, continuing to stroke her hair and speak softly to her as Greg Cameron began slowly undoing the rough bandage.

"Except for the little guy with the scorpion sting, the others have the usual childhood cuts and bruises," Greg said as he unraveled the gauze covering. "One's got a mild fever, which I'll check out in a moment."

His voice went on, quietly switching to Spanish to reassure the little girl, and then back to English as the patient stiffened in pain. Suddenly, the little girl screeched in agony, and Brooke felt a rush of nausea as the pungent smell of infection reached her.

"I'll do what I can, but she should go back to the States with us if we can arrange it."

"That bad?" Brooke asked, slowly turning her head to see. Instantly, she wished she hadn't. She flinched involuntarily but forced herself to keep her face from showing her reaction. Then she turned back to the girl whose body was now contorted in pain.

"Oh, Greg!" Brooke said softly.

"Now," he said gently, reaching for his bag, "you see why I work with children?"

"Yes," Brooke breathed. "I also see why you try to keep from getting emotionally attached to your patients."

After Greg had rebandaged the wound, Brooke left the infirmary area so he could examine the boy's scorpion bite. No one greeted her as she made her way back through the orphanage, so she stepped outside for some fresh air. Her thoughts immediately focused on this new side of Greg Cameron that she had seen for the first time. He was a soft, gentle man who loved children. Her eyes welled with tears as she pondered his compassion.

Brooke was suddenly aware that some of the children were standing at a respectful distance, watching her. Quickly, she dried her eyes and smiled, forcing herself to think of other things besides the children in the infirmary.

Her eyes swept across the western horizon, which contained one of the most spectacular sunsets she had ever seen. She was startled by some dark, ominous, thunderheads and lightning to the north. Brooke had forgotten that violent storms sprang up from time to time over the desert area; she hoped Scotty's plane wasn't caught in the bad weather.

It was almost dark when Greg stepped outside the orphanage and walked over to the fig trees where she was standing.

"Everything OK?" she asked.

He nodded. "Except for that little girl. I hope we'll have room for her to go back to San Francisco in Carla's plane."

Brooke nodded and changed the subject with a note of concern in her voice. "Greg, it's time Scotty was back. In fact, he should have been here a long time ago. You don't suppose he ran into more trouble trying to get Pepe off . . . ?"

"Don't worry, Brooke. Scotty probably took Pepe back to Guerrero Negro and decided it was too late to fly back here. Without telephones or any way of communicating, we just have to assume that no news is good news."

As they watched the continuous flash of lightning in the northern sky, Brooke saw Hernando and a young Mexican running toward them.

Hernando waved his hands at the anxious-appearing young man and began a long, breathless discourse in Spanish.

After Hernando had finished, Greg explained to Brooke. "There's an emergency in a remote village at the end of the Vizcaino Desert. That young man," Greg pointed, "says his wife is dying in childbirth. They saw the plane and figured a doctor would be here. I've got to go."

Brooke made an instant decision. "I'll go with you!"

Greg tried to get her to stay and rest, but Brooke was terrified at the idea of being alone with people with whom she couldn't communicate.

"We don't have time to stand here arguing," Greg admitted. "Come on with us."

It was getting colder, and the lightning still flashed in the distance; the direction they would have to travel, Brooke learned. While Greg hurried to get his bag and a coat, Brooke used hand motions to tell Hernando and the distraught father-to-be to bring a can of boiled ham, a box of crackers, a small, sharp knife, and the two five-gallon cans of water Scotty had thoughtfully left behind for her.

Greg returned with his bag and two coats. "Here," he said, tossing her one, "it's not a good fit, but it's better than your sweater."

He looked doubtfully at the dilapidated dusty car, which the young man had driven to Soledad in, and asked Hernando if there was a better vehicle around. There was, the *jefe* replied with a smile, a very good American Jeep a friend would be glad to loan them.

Hernando once again took off on the run and

returned about seven or eight minutes later in the driver's seat of the four-wheel-drive vehicle. Brooke was relieved to see it had a canvas top and plastic side curtains. The water and food were loaded into the Jeep, along with extra gasoline. Greg made sure there was a jack and a spare tire. They said a quick good-bye to Hernando, and then they were off.

For about an hour, they bounced dangerously fast along a rutted dirt road. Brooke began to feel car sick from all the violent jostling as the Jeep's lights burrowed a weak path through the dust raised by their guide's car. Then suddenly the taillights ahead stood still, and Greg pulled the Jeep up alongside the rolling junk heap. Steam poured from the radiator and spewed from under the hood.

Greg listened to their guide's rapid explosion of Spanish and turned to Brooke. "He's busted a water hose. I was afraid something like this might happen! The guide says it's not far, and he will walk because we've got all that stuff in the back. It's just over those hills, he says, and we can't miss the place. So hang on; we've got a baby to deliver, *pronto!*"

The sturdy little vehicle leaped ahead, the lights drilling a hole straight into the black night.

"Keep a sharp eye out for lights." Greg said as he turned to Brooke. "That'd be the village. If we miss those weak kerosene lamps, we'll end up in the Vizcaino Desert, and that's no place for a couple of *gringos* to get lost!"

Chapter Twelve

The blackness of the Baja night had startled Brooke. She could see nothing as she peered off into the distance looking for signs of civilization. She couldn't even pick up the faint silhouette of rocky hills flanking the road. She had shivered when she thought of what it would be like to be wandering in that desert without the security of the Jeep's bouncing headlights. It had been a great relief when the night had yielded a pinpoint of light, then another ... and another.

Greg stopped and pounded on the door of the first dwelling they had come to. A quick conversation had resulted in directions to the pregnant mother's house, and within minutes, the doctor was at the patient's side.

It had been a difficult delivery, but before dawn, a baby girl and her young mother were facing their first day together.

Greg and Brooke had graciously refused all offers of rest and hospitality; they had received grateful handshakes and hugs and accepted exclamations of *hermano* and *hermana*, brother and sister. These must be Christians, Brooke assumed, because they thought Greg and Brooke were part of the Christian medical team, which periodically flew down from *Los Estados Unidos* to help their brothers and sisters in Christ south of the border.

Brooke's unreasoning fears of the night before were gone. In the bright September morning, everything looked good! Brooke looked closely at Greg Cameron as he prepared to disengage the Jeep's clutch and realized he looked worn and ragged.

"Want me to drive, Greg?"

He shook his head. The curl, which fell over his forehead and down toward the eye, was matted with water from when he'd washed after the delivery.

"No, thanks. It's not far. Even that fellow who came for us was able to walk from his broken-down car to the village in a few hours. The Jeep'll get us there in time for breakfast. You hungry?"

"Starved, now that you mention it."

"Reach back there and grab something. I could use a little nourishment, myself."

Brooke fussed with opening the canned ham until Greg showed her a tab and key. "You'd make someone a good nurse, Brooke, but I'm not sure that opening cans is your strong point."

He said it soberly, but she sensed he was teasing her. "You were wonderful back there," she said softly. "That girl would have died without your help."

"You the medical expert in this vehicle, Miss Brooke Summers?"

She looked confidently at him. "Expert enough to know that both the mother and baby might not have made it without your help."

He was smiling, she thought, well, almost. "You ever going to tell me about yourself?" she asked, watching the desert slide by the bouncing Jeep's closed sides. It was still chilly in spite of the bright sun.

He turned to look at her. "Would it make any difference?"

Would it? No, not really. Only one thing seemed to matter now: that he care for her. But there was nothing concrete on which to hang Brooke's hope, nothing solid enough for her. And yet . . .

"Not really, I guess. But I am curious, Greg. Every time I ask you that question, I get the impression you are running away from something, or hiding something from your past."

Brooke noticed Greg shift uncomfortably in his seat, and she could see that his neck and face were turning red. She wasn't quite sure how he was going to respond.

"You know, I was really disappointed with you when you asked me those questions on your newscast," he finally answered. "I knew you were out to embarrass me in front of your viewers."

There he goes changing the subject again, Brooke thought as she planned her defense.

"Greg, I had good reason for my actions," she began.

"And you're a woman of strong convictions, right? Nothing ever gets in your way when you decide what's best for Brooke Summers; that right? It doesn't matter who you hurt to get where you're going, does it?"

Greg's sarcasm surprised Brooke. He had accused her of being selfish and egotistical, and she could not let his questions go unanswered. She did her best to control her rising anger as she responded.

"My father always taught me that the world was out there, just waiting for me to claim what part I wanted. But I have also learned that nobody is going to give me anything; at least, none of the things I really want."

"And what do you really want, Brooke?"

"What do I want?" She pondered. *Heartbeat. A new contract. Top ratings. Perhaps someday even a national television shot. Her brother to grow up and face responsibilities.* And—

"You're not answering," Greg reminded her.

"Oh, I was just thinking."

"About what you really want?"

"Yes." Good! He wasn't getting headlong into a fight with her. She handed him the crackers and offered the opened tin of ham. "You want some?"

"Not the crackers," he said. "Dan Roberts will tell you that stuff turns to glue around your teeth and becomes pure sugar. Terrible for your teeth; great for the dentist.

"Incidentally, Dan told me on the flight down why all the women seem to be missing their front teeth. There's so much dental trouble that they figure it's easier to have their teeth pulled when one starts acting up.

"Once, Dan said, a girl without tooth problems insisted he pull hers while he was there. He made her wait until all the other patients were helped, then—because she was still waiting and wanted—he consented to pull her teeth."

Brooke nodded in understanding. "Well, fortunately, I've got my own teeth and I don't think eating a few crackers will hurt them."

"Hey!" Greg said, changing the subject. "I had forgotten all about the thunder and lightning we saw last night."

Greg braked their vehicle at the top of the small rise, and they watched their tracks from the night before disappear into a dark and wet wash.

He braked the vehicle at the top of a small rise. They saw their tracks from the night before disappear into a dark and wet wash.

"Flash flood must have passed through here," Greg said. "I'll ease down and see if we can creep across."

The front wheels touched the edge of the dark spot and started to sink. Greg jammed the vehicle into reverse and backed out immediately. The engine whined as the wheels spun them back onto solid ground.

"That's mud—not sand!" Greg shouted. "Can't cross there! We'd better take a walk and see if there's a way around."

"I'm getting sleepy," Brooke said as they got out and walked carefully along the wash. "All that food and a night without sleep."

"Me, too." Greg took her hand and helped her over some small boulders. "But as soon as we clear this little obstacle, we'll be almost back to

Soledad and there we can catch some sleep."

"I don't know," Brooke said doubtfully. "I've got to get some footage shot. Assuming, of course, that Scotty's back with Pepe and the others."

They came to a small hill, which gave them a view to their left. Brooke's heart stirred at the sight of a deep, barren canyon too wild and broken to cross. "Well," she said, "how about the other direction?"

They walked back, passed the Jeep, and climbed another hill. Greg sighed. "Guess those dunes over there look like our best bet. The Jeep should climb them without any trouble if they're as solid as what we're walking on here."

"You mean—leave the trail?"

"We can't stay here and wait for that mud to dry. It may take days. And there's no place for a plane to land in this rolling area."

"But? When I was a little girl, the first thing I learned at camp was: 'Don't leave the trail and you won't get lost.' "

Greg shrugged. "True, of course. But if we keep the sun on our left—where it is now—we should be able to circle around the little canyons and cross at some rocky creek bed. If not, we'll follow our tracks back here to this point and wait it out. OK?"

She sighed. "I guess."

They returned to the Jeep and Greg squinted toward the sun; then he turned the Jeep to the right. It climbed easily up the solid-packed sand dunes.

He turned to grin at her. "May as well catch a few winks now if you can, Brooke. I'll keep this baby from bouncing any more than necessary."

"Let's wait till we get around these endless rolling dunes," she replied.

"Suit yourself."

They drove for half an hour, periodically veering off to one side or the other to avoid boulders or washes that were dry but too rough to cross. Brooke watched the sun seemingly change directions, but each time, Greg brought it back into position on their left. Satisfied that they were rolling smoothly on hard-packed ground toward Soledad, Brooke leaned her head against Greg's shoulder and closed her eyes.

It felt so good to be close to him! He had been so gentle with the frightened mother whose child had been delivered after such a hard night. Brooke had felt sorry for the woman and her anxious family. Then there had been the cry of the newborn child. . . .

With a start, Brooke opened her eyes and sat up. Her neck was stiff from leaning against Greg. He had stopped the vehicle and was looking at the sun through the fingers of his cupped hands.

"What's the matter?" Brooke asked.

"Time for some water," he replied.

She poured some water into a collapsible tin cup he produced from his bag. "Old habit," he apologized. "I carry all kinds of curious little things with me." He was rummaging through the glove box.

"What're you looking for?"

"A map."

"A map?"

"Yes. See those tracks over there?" He pointed.

Brooke's eyes followed his hand. She nodded. "They're ours."

"Ours?"

"Made an hour or so ago."

"Are you sure?"

"I'm sure." He said it in such a resigned, quiet way that it made her spill her remaining cup of water into the sand.

"You mean—we're—?"

He interrupted. "Now don't get upset! I just want to check a map. But I can't seem to find one."

Brooke managed a shaky laugh of disbelief. "Greg, don't try to scare me."

"We should've spotted the *Laguna Ojo de Liebre* by now. But we haven't."

Brooke tried to keep her voice calm. "How could we have gotten lost when it's such a short distance? I mean, that man whose car broke down walked into the village in a few hours! We're in a Jeep, and—."

She paused, looking at him. Slowly, she finished her own sentence, but not the way she'd intended.

"And we're lost, aren't we? Really lost?"

Shaking his head, Greg said somberly, "I guess I was just too sleepy or exhausted from last night. There's no way I should have gotten lost, but—" He shrugged, looking over the desert.

Brooke's eyes followed his. She hadn't noticed it before, but the sun had shifted to their right. They had no other visible guide; the desert was one vast rolling series of barren hills. Even the little ravine, which had brought the flash flood, was gone. She looked at the tire tracks some feet off to her left.

"We're going in circles, aren't we, Greg?"

He nodded.

"How big is this desert?"

He turned away.

"Greg, is it as vast as it appeared from the air?"

"No need to be alarmed, Brooke. We've got food and water. And three airplanes will be looking for us pretty soon, if we don't turn up."

Brooke wanted to cry, *If Scotty didn't have more trouble! Maybe they're out looking for him!* But instead, she said quietly, "What do we do now?"

He took a deep breath. "We can either keep trying to find our way back, or we can wait. But there's no place to land a plane here."

Brooke's fear flared into an angry question. "How could you have gotten us lost?"

His eyes turned black. Angrily and silently, he whirled about and started walking rapidly across the firm, brown sand.

"Greg! Where are you going?"

He didn't answer; he just kept walking.

Chapter Thirteen

Brooke followed Greg as he stomped across the hot desert sands away from the Jeep. She hadn't meant to lash out at him, but the combination of fatigue and frustration had left her temper vulnerable. She regretted having made him the scapegoat for their dilemma.

"I'm sorry, Greg," she said nervously, coming up to where he had stopped on a small, sandy mesa. "I had no right to blame you."

He surprised her. Brooke had expected a violent tongue lashing from a man who could be quite volatile. But his dark eyes were soft, and he was calm as he turned to respond.

"I was confident we would find our way when we left the trail. But I was wrong. You deserve to know why."

She laid a hand on his. "You don't need to explain anything, Greg. I should have stayed awake and helped."

He shook his head. "I guess now I know how Jonah felt."

She blinked. "Jonah?"

"Yes. You remember the story?"

"It's been a long time, but I remember the whale—or fish—and all that. I don't understand what you mean."

"Remember how Jonah got into all his trouble?"

Brooke hesitated. "God wanted him to do something— Oh, I remember! God wanted Jonah to go to Nineveh, but Jonah didn't want to do it. So he got on a boat headed in the opposite direction. That's when he was tossed overboard and swallowed."

"There was a terrible storm," Greg said softly, looking over the endless, empty horizon. "Jonah recognized that he was the cause of all the other people's trouble on that ship, so he offered to let them throw him overboard."

He paused; his eyes filled with pain. He pulled his hand free of Brooke's and ran it thoughtfully over his mouth and chin. Brooke heard the dark stubble of his day-old beard.

"I don't think I'm following you," she said.

"Brooke, this is hard to admit," he said with a forced smile. "But I'm sort of a Jonah in a Jeep."

She tensed. "You're not making sense, Greg!"

He turned toward her, his dark eyes cloudy with some inner emotion clearly visible to her. "Brooke, several times you've asked me about my past, and I've always sidestepped the issue. Now you need to know the truth. I've been a man on the run."

"On the run! What do you mean, Greg? Have

you done something wrong?"

"Oh, I'm not in trouble with the law," he answered with a slight note of humor in his voice. "In fact, other than a handful of speeding tickets, I don't think I've ever done anything illegal.

"I mean, on the run from God. I think there may have been a reason why I got lost out here in this desolate place. There are no distractions to keep me from listening to God. But I feel badly that you've gotten dragged into this."

Brooke ignored his comment about her and spoke up. "Why should God have to deal with you?"

Greg did not reply to her question. During the silence, Brooke couldn't help but think of the irony of their situation. Here they were, two intelligent, sophisticated people who seemed to be doing just fine without bringing religion into their lives. Now, they were talking about God with the quiet assurance that he existed; talking about him as if he were as real as the vast, empty Vizcaino Desert, which held them prisoners.

Greg slowly turned around, surveying the full hundred and eighty degrees of endless desert and bleak horizon. When he had returned to his original position, he sighed.

"I wonder if the great fish that swallowed Jonah had a name?" he mused.

"Greg, you're talking nonsense! What possible difference does the name of Jonah's fish make?"

"Because," Greg answered softly, "the whale that swallowed you and me does have a name: Vizcaino Desert."

Brooke said nothing as she watched the secretive, mysterious quality that had always been so much a part of Dr. Greg Cameron return. He had withdrawn into himself again.

He led the way back to the Jeep, and she followed, fighting mixed emotions, including a spreading stain of fear about his emotional health.

They drove on, trying to estimate the sun's earlier position in relation to where it was now. That was next to impossible, because it had almost circumnavigated the entire sky. Dusk was no more than three hours away. Sleep tugged at both their bodies, and twice Brooke realized she'd almost fallen asleep sitting up.

The Jeep crawled down a little hill while drifting sand raced ahead of the vehicle. "Wind's coming up," Greg observed. "Going to be cold tonight."

"You think we'll still be stuck out here tonight?"

"I think we'll do our best to get out of here before then, but unless we do better than we've been—" His words broke off as the Jeep suddenly seemed to be stopped by an invisible hand.

"Greg! What is it?"

"Deep, loose sand. We're stuck!" He shifted rapidly, trying to free the little vehicle, but all four wheels quickly dug themselves further down into the soft sand.

"Here," he said, sliding out onto the ground. "You take the wheel and let me see if I can push us out. Put it in reverse and slowly hit the accelerator. We get those wheels spinning too fast and they'll just sink deeper. So be careful."

They worked hard, but the vehicle was

hopelessly trapped by the sand. At last Greg called, "It's no use! Ease off!" He came puffing to stand beside her, his hands scratched and bleeding, his clothes dirty. Perspiration streaked his dark face.

"Oh, Greg! What'll we do?"

"I'll look in the backseat and see what I can find to dig us out. You scout around and see if there are any brush, small rocks, or sticks—anything we can place under the drive wheels to get traction. And remember to watch out for snakes and scorpions."

Fearfully aware that sidewinders (the pale-colored rattlesnakes found in the desert) could bury all but their eyes and nostrils in the sand, which so perfectly matched their camouflage, Brooke found a few small rocks. She returned to the vehicle to see Greg digging sand from under the rear wheels with the tire iron.

"That's all I could find," he panted, stopping to rest. "Looks as though you didn't find much of use, either."

"I did the best I could!" Brooke snapped back sarcastically.

"Easy, now!" He stood up, brushing fine sand from his hands and clothes. The sand was snatched by the rising wind and whipped away across the desolation. "We've been through this before. You're tired. I'm tired. It's not going to help a bit if we get upset again."

She nodded and took a deep breath. "What can I do?"

"Soon as I pack those rocks under these wheels, we'll try rocking it out. You know: shift back and forth real fast. And if it starts moving backward, keep it going. Don't stop until we're back on solid ground. OK?"

They worked rocking the car for thirty minutes. Repeatedly the Jeep's motor wound up, the wheels spun, Greg yelled, and Brooke eased off on the accelerator. As they were all set to try again, Brooke heard a strange noise and looked in panic at the flat hood.

"Greg! Steam!"

"We're boiling! You didn't watch the temperature gauge!"

"How'd I know to do that?"

"Anyone knows that much."

"Not quite. I'm not used to getting myself out when I'm stuck!"

Their brief exchange halted abruptly as the steam rose alarmingly. Greg raised the flat hood and jumped back as dark brown water suddenly erupted skyward.

"Now we've done it," Greg said as the radiator spewed hot, ugly liquid into the wind, which then blew it across the sand.

They watched helplessly until the eruption had subsided. Brooke broke the silence as the two stood staring at the wet sand. "Now what?"

Greg pondered for a moment before he responded. "Two choices. We can pour some water in from our fresh supply and try getting out of here, or we can leave the Jeep as it is and hope somebody finds us."

Brooke thought aloud. "If we use the drinking water, we may run short for ourselves. But if we abandon the Jeep, we certainly won't be able to walk out of here. Those two big water jugs will be much too awkward to carry. And if we stay here, and nobody comes—"

"Hey, sundown will be here shortly," Greg in

terrupted. "You've seen how black it gets here at night. Suppose we wash up a little, have something to eat, and think about the best course of action?"

"You mean—spend the night here?"

"I'll sleep on the hood. It's been done before to avoid the scorpions and rattlesnakes on the ground. You can close the side curtains and be fairly warm inside the Jeep."

"Couldn't we build a fire?"

"With what? You couldn't even find enough brush to put under the wheels."

"I tried!" Brooke exclaimed, fighting her fear, which was manifesting itself as anger.

"Remember what I said about getting upset?"

"Who's getting upset?"

"You're losing your temper, Brooke." Greg's voice rose sharply and the dark eyes flashed with anger. "You're starting to get emotional, and that's the last thing we need right now."

"You're pretty quick to condemn," she flared. "Considering that you got us into this."

He opened his mouth to make a sharp, bitter reply, then stopped. Slowly, he nodded. "Yes," he admitted. "I told you it's my fault, and why. Now, let's try and think rationally about our problem and our alternatives."

Brooke calmed down as they discussed their problem as if there were alternative solutions. They could drive at night, but they might get lost even deeper in the desert. There was also the danger of running into something that might wreck a tire or get them stuck in another spot.

"It's agreed, then, Brooke?" Greg asked. "We spend the night here?"

Brooke looked at the Jeep, still twisted slightly sideways in the sand. "We stay here," she agreed. "Tomorrow morning we'll decide what to do about the water."

"Good thinking," he said. He pulled out one big jug of water and held it while she wet her hands and the large handkerchief he'd produced. She wiped some of the grime off her face and felt the fine sand grind into her pores.

"I'm going to be a mess when we get out of here," she said with forced cheerfulness. "The way my face is getting scratched up, I won't be able to go before the cameras for a week."

"You're face is beautiful," he said quietly.

She looked up into his dark eyes. The beard was a strong black smear now, heavily splattered with mud where the perspiration had turned the fine sand into a paste. "Thank you," she said.

They finished washing in silence. Greg shook the water jug and listened to it with his head cocked to one side. "We used more than I thought," he said. "Probably be a good idea to begin rationing ourselves."

Her fear oozed out again, a tight, gripping tension, which threatened to cut off her breath. "What happens if we use up all our water?"

"We'll get out of here before then. Or someone will find us."

"But if we don't, and nobody comes?"

He pursed his lips and reached for the ham "This meat is really salty, which is good. Salt helps combat dehydration, you know?"

"You didn't answer my question, Greg."

He held the canned ham in his hand and studied her a moment before answering. "Med ically, a person can live about seventy-two hours without water. After that, the victim becomes comatose."

"You mean, the unconsciousness that precedes death?"

"Yes. You see, the electrolytes go crazy, speaking from a layman's point of view—"

She interrupted. "Never mind! I get the picture. You're saying that we can live about three days after our water runs out."

"That's what I'm saying."

"Well," she said with a sudden flash of confidence, "there's no way we're going to be lost that long!"

"So you've cast your vote already, have you, Brooke? In the morning, we put water in the radiator to keep the engine from overheating, and drive on—assuming, of course, we can get out of that sand."

"Why not?" She forced herself to be cheerful. "Why not, indeed?"

They ate sparingly of the ham, drank carefully of their water, and then bundled up for the night. It was surprisingly cold, even inside the Jeep. Brooke felt sorry for Greg, curled up on the Jeep's hood with an old sack under his head and his neck tucked into his jacket.

All was quiet, except for the occasional howl of a coyote in the distance. The darkness of the night loomed blacker than Brooke thought possible. She was used to seeing the glow of city lights in the sky. But on this moonless night, she could barely see the hand in front of her nose.

As weary as she was, sleep did not come easily. She tossed and turned for nearly an hour, trying to find a comfortable position. But her mind could not refrain from worrying about what the next day might bring. Then she leaned against the passenger's door and let her eyes look up through the bug-splattered windshield. Overhead was one of the most spectacular displays of stars Brooke had ever seen.

Astronomy was a subject she knew little about, but she did remember a few things from a junior high science class. She noticed a fairly wide band of white stretching across the top of the sky—the Milky Way. She remembered once hearing that earth revolved around a small star in the huge galaxy's tip. The light from some of the stars took hundreds and thousands of years to reach earth across the great chasm of space. Brooke pictured the earth as a tiny dot on the map of the universe. Suddenly she shivered, but not from the cool night chill. Her lips moved, but the words were soundless. *Oh, Lord, it's been a while since I've talked to you, but I know you're listening. When I look at the immensity of your universe, I realize how small and insignificant I am. Yet, when I feel my fingers, I know they are different from anyone else's. You created me as a unique individual.*

I know most of us only look to you when the going gets tough. But still I ask you to help us get out of this barren desert.

Her lips stopped moving but she kept looking out at the stars and thought about how alone they were. She knew God had indeed listened. Her anxiety about the next day began to fade.

Brooke took one last look at the canopy of stars overhead. Then, she closed her eyes with a surprising peace, and slept soundly for the first time in almost two days.

Chapter Fourteen

As soon as it was light enough to see, Greg started digging around the Jeep's wheels with the tire iron. Brooke then followed Greg's instructions closely as he once again rocked the Jeep back and forth. Finally the doctor, turned temporary engineer, stood with a satisfied grin as the little vehicle spun its way out of the sandy grooves and once again idled on solid ground.

"Well," Greg said, tossing the tire iron onto the backseat, "that'll never be my favorite shovel, but I'm glad we had it, just the same."

Brooke looked at the one remaining can of water. "We used an awful lot for that radiator," she said thoughtfully.

"Had to. Remember? When the radiator blew up yesterday almost every drop ended up in the sand. But we should be OK now. You want to drive?"

"No, I don't think so. But I do have a suggestion," Brooke added. "We should have a plan so we don't waste gasoline."

"I thought about that during the night. We can either try to retrace our tracks—which is hard because we can't see them in some places—or we can try to find a high, level place where a plane could land, and just wait there. What do you think?"

Brooke hesitated, then replied, "Why not both?"

Greg nodded. "My thinking, too. We'll hope to find our way back to the road. If not, as soon as the tank is almost empty, we'll scout for a good potential landing strip and wait."

Everything went fine as morning progressed toward noon. When the tire tracks from the day before seemed to disappear, Brooke was able to see where they started again. Then, one time they weren't so lucky. Brooke and Greg both got out and walked, cutting back and forth across the hard-packed desert soil. But the tracks were nowhere in sight. They returned to the Jeep and rolled up the side curtains to cool off in the shade made by the canvas roof.

"May as well eat something," Greg said, reaching for the ham. "I'm beginning to hate this stuff, but it's better than nothing." He sliced a piece and gave it to her on a cracker.

They ate without conversation astounded by the incredible silence of the desert. The wind had not come up, and the only sound was the hood of the Jeep cooling off now that the engine had been turned off.

Brooke found herself fighting fear. That morning, when the desert was cool, she had felt hopeful. Especially when she remembered the comforting feeling she had felt as she fell asleep the night before. But now, she could see waves of heat rising off the sandy floor in the distance. The Jeep seemed like an oven as the sun beat down at well over 100 degrees.

Fear was an insidious thing, she knew. It oozed through her entire being and slowly began taking control of her mind. Her normal instinct said, "Attack! Maneuver your way out of your predicament." But there was nothing she could do. Her adversary was a vast, lifeless desert, which had already swallowed them up and erased their tire tracks.

With an effort, Brooke spoke. "Greg, I wish you'd explain how you are 'running away from God.' "

He swallowed the last bite of cracker and wiped his fingers on a piece of dirty cloth he'd found on the backseat. "You mean why I'm like Jonah?"

"That, and how you come to speak Spanish so well."

He stiffened, and Brooke felt an instant reaction of anger.

"Listen, Greg," she snapped, "if you are going to tell me that we're stuck out here because you've been playing games with God, then the least you can do is explain what you mean."

"Shh!" He held up a restraining hand, his body tensing even more.

Brooke realized fear was forcing her to lash out, but she seemed powerless to stop. "Don't shush me! I'm getting sick of your—"

"Listen, I said!" His voice snapped so sharply against her ears that she drew back.

Greg leaped from the Jeep and ran out to one side, peering at the sky with both hands shading his eyes.

"Greg, what is it?"

"I thought I heard . . ." He left the sentence unfinished as he spun slowly in a circle, searching the hot, empty sky.

"A plane?" Brooke leaped from the Jeep and started searching the sky. She cocked her head and listened until the silence seemed to ring loudly in her ears. Angrily, she turned to face him. "You are driving me crazy with your tactics!"

"My tactics?" His voice was seeping with annoyance. "You think the worst of me, don't you?" He walked quickly toward her, his dark beard glistening with perspiration. "I thought I heard a plane! Only you wouldn't keep quiet long enough for me to make sure!"

"Oh, so now it's my fault?"

"Brooke, you're by far the most aggravating woman I've ever met! I used to admire your spunk. But now I find your abrasiveness particularly offensive."

She tried to think of a retort, but her fear and anger was so intense she turned in bristling silence to the Jeep. She reached inside and pulled the water can over so hard she slopped some of it onto the sand.

"Hey! Watch what you're doing!"

Again, Brooke wanted to reply, but her feelings were so intense she couldn't speak. She poured herself a drink, letting some of it run down her chin. She put the lid back on the can and got stiffly and silently into the passenger's seat.

Wordlessly, Greg took the wheel and slammed the vehicle into gear. He drove fast across the trackless desert for a few minutes, and then when his boiling emotions cooled to a simmer, he slowed down.

"No sense wasting gasoline by driving hard," he said quietly. "I'll ease along and we'll both look for tracks. OK?"

She nodded, still angry, but she was also fearful, and didn't want to fight with him. Not now, especially.

They drove through the afternoon without finding their tracks. Neither did they find a high, open, and level spot where a plane might land. Near sundown, he stopped and stepped down from the driver's seat. The hot desert wind dried the beads of sweat, which had formed on his brow.

"May as well pour in the last of the gasoline," he said, reaching into the backseat.

The next thing Brooke heard was a sharp, sudden breath, and she whirled to see what the problem was. Greg lifted the water can, and she thought for a moment he'd mistaken it for the gasoline can. But when she saw the horrified expression on his face, she knew something was wrong with the water.

"Brooke," he said sharply, "you didn't put the cap on right! Look!" He held up the last water container and shook it vigorously.

Brooke's heart sank at the slight sound of the water. She turned fully in the seat so she could see the container. But even before he spoke, she knew the truth.

"Almost all leaked out," he said with controlled anger. "Almost every bit is wasted!"

The sun went down on their hostility, but their antagonism toward each other had not abated. Brooke wanted to blame Greg for making her angry and careless, but she knew she had no one to blame but herself. She'd wasted almost all of their water, and now the prospect of death from thirst was much closer and very real. They would only have enough water left for a couple of swallows each for one or two days."

Greg poured the last of the gasoline into the tank and got back in the Jeep. "We'd better find that high, open place tomorrow," he said without elaboration. "Meantime, we'd better plan on spending another night in this desert."

Brooke's anger had given way once again to a rising tide of fear. She was fighting hard to control it, but the terror of death seemed so real and so close she could not decide what to say. She nodded, and Greg drove to a sheltered side of a dry sand dune to cut down the wind, which was rising hard, carrying fine grains of almost invisible sand that seemed determined to pit their windshield.

The strained silence between them seemed to get heavier as darkness settled quickly and quietly upon them. Wordlessly, Greg took his jacket and his burlap sack pillow and climbed upon the hood to sleep.

Brooke was miserable. She sat stiffly in her seat for a long time, watching the stars come out and the terrible blackness of the night engulf them. The late-afternoon wind had given way to an eerie calm.

Countdown, she told herself, had begun—a countdown of the last hours. She shuddered and

drew herself up inside the sweater she'd
brought, and the extra coat Greg had given her.
She didn't feel sleepy, but the utter stillness
slowly lulled her into nodding. She made herself as comfortable as possible and yielded herself to sleep.

She wasn't sure how long she had slept when
she was suddenly startled to consciousness.
The scream seemed so close that it made every
inch of her body a mass of gooseflesh.

Through the windshield, she saw Greg sit up.

The scream came again. Brooke was so
frightened she couldn't even call out.

Greg turned slowly and said softly, "Turn on
the headlights."

Still feeling gooseflesh chase itself all over
her arms, she fumbled for the switch. The lights
bore a hole in the blackness, and there, perhaps
twenty yards in front of the Jeep, shined two of
the most piercing eyes Brooke had ever seen.
Brooke shivered as what she guessed was a
cougar stood motionless in the light.

"It's OK, Brooke," Greg said, his voice coming
past the windshield and into the side curtains,
which she'd let down to keep out the night cold.
"He's probably never seen anything like this
Jeep, or maybe even a human. Hit the horn."

She obeyed, her mouth dry. The big cat turned
and bounded away into the night, his long tail
twitching behind.

When the lights had been switched off and the
silent, black night again swallowed them up,
Brooke wanted to get out of the Jeep and go to
Greg. But he lay down again, snuggled deep into
his coat, and soon was snoring lightly.

Brooke was angry with him. Didn't he care

enough to comfort her? Why didn't he hold her in his arms? But then, Brooke asked herself sadly, why should he?

She tried to sleep again, but she was fearfully awake, expecting the big cat to scream again. She remembered that cougars were supposed to be among the most cowardly of animals, but that was small comfort.

She huddled into her sweater and coat, and tried to pray like she had the night before. Only this time there was no sense of God's majesty and power. Not really knowing what to say, she slipped again into restless sleep.

Chapter Fifteen

It was late the next afternoon when they came to
a high stretch of flat, open sand. The Jeep made
no tracks, Brooke saw, glancing behind her as
Greg eased the vehicle to a stop.

"We don't have enough gasoline left to go on,"
he said quietly. "So we may as well stay here
and hope they fly over us tomorrow."

Brooke looked at his profile. He wasn't looking at her, but swept his gaze over the possible
landing strip. "Yes," she said, "I guess this is
where we'd better wait."

Sleep came easier that night, and soon she
dreamed that Scotty's plane was circling overhead. Scotty brought the craft in for a landing,
and was soon running toward her. When they
met, he swept her up into his arms.

"Oh, Brooke!" he whispered. "We've been
searching for you almost every minute of day-

light. I was afraid we wouldn't find you in time."

Brooke strained to hear Scotty's next words, but then realized they weren't going to come. She was awake inside the dirty Jeep. The desert night was black as ever, and her heart pounded with disappointment.

Through the windshield, she could see Greg's dark shadow curled up on the uncomfortably short hood of the Jeep. How could he sleep so soundly in the midst of danger that made her mind turn to a molten jelly of fear?

"Oh, Lord!" she murmured, her voice so low it did not disturb Greg, "help us!"

She wanted to pray more, but the words didn't come. Instead, a rebellion began to form in her mind.

It wasn't right for them to die like this! They were both young. Neither had ever been married; they left no children. They had not even really known life. Now they were dying of thirst, alone and angry with each other, in the silent, vast expanses of the Vizcaino Desert.

She licked her cracked and dried lips and felt a slight twitch of pain. Her mouth, her whole body, seemed to cry out for water. But there was none. Her angry carelessness had robbed them of precious fluid, and started their rush toward death.

Why am I in this mess? she wordlessly asked herself. *Why . . . ?"*

She began to think once again of the reasons she had come to Baja. Heartbeat. A higher audience share. Anything to further her career. All of that was more important to her than the love of a man. She knew Scotty loved her, but she was far from ready to love him.

She had thought she was falling in love with Dr. Gregory Cameron. But she had done almost everything she knew to destroy that love. And why? The painful truth hit her hard.

"My career," she said softly aloud, "is more important than anything at all. Not that a girl shouldn't have a career, but . . ." She paused before she said it . . . "at this price?"

She shook her head and felt tears close to her eyes. She blinked them back and looked through the windshield at Greg. He had his own ghosts to fight; yet he fought them alone, without her, even as death loomed so close to them.

He moved in his sleep, turning so he seemed to be on his back. The light snoring stopped, and for a moment, Brooke thought he had awakened. But he did not move, and her thoughts were lifted to the stars.

At first, the tiny flecks of white seemed far away. Then, as Brooke readjusted her focus, they appeared almost close enough to touch in that black, black night. Brooke recognized Orion, the Dog Star, and the Big Dipper. She even found what she thought was the Little Dipper, a constellation she knew could never be seen in the lighted sky over the Bay area.

How much of the beautiful parts of life I've forgotten, she realized, *as I pushed so hard to succeed. Now all that's really important is living.*

Brooke reached out for the only one who could share this moment with her. *Lord, I took all of life—all I wanted, but . . ."* She shook her head, fighting tears. . . . *where has it gotten me with you?*

Her prayer continued: the quiet sobs buried within her. *Father, somewhere in Psalms I re-*

*member a verse that says if we delight in you, you
will give us the desires of our hearts. I don't feel like
I deserve any of this, but I'm going to be honest with
you. I want some things that didn't seem all that
important until the last couple days. I want a hus-
band, and children, and–yes–I want to serve you. I
want to live, Lord!*

*Help Scotty to find us–tomorrow–before it's too
late.*

She began to weep softly, the tears seeping
out the corner of her eyes and down her cheeks.
Slowly, still staring at the sky, she closed her
eyes and was soon resting in a deep sleep.

She dreamed she was in Hawaii, where she'd
been with her parents as a teenager. But this
time she was with Greg Cameron, and he was
offering her a tall, frosted glass of something
exotic and beautiful. There were pineapple
spears sticking up out of the pink liquid, with a
tiny blue umbrella shading a bright red mara-
schino cherry. The liquid was cool on her lips
and tongue, before sliding down her throat.
Then she was laughing, running toward a waterfall lined with green ferns and wild, tiny orchids.

Greg reached up and plucked one of the tiny
orchids and handed it to her with a smile.
Brooke looked at her yellow and red Hawaiian
print garment and saw there were no pockets.
She looked uncertainly up into Greg's handsome face.

"Put it in your hair," he said.

"Of course!" she exclaimed. "But which side
shall I wear it on? I've forgotten: If a local
wahine wears a blossom in the right side of her
hair, it means she's single and available. No

wait! Maybe that's the side that means she's married. I'm all mixed up!"

Greg laughed, gently and tenderly, as his dark eyes glowed softly with love. Her heart began to beat louder, matching the thunder of the waterfall, as he reached out and took Brooke's hand. Slowly, he raised her fingers to his lips.

"Oh, Brooke!" he whispered huskily, "I love you so!" His hands reached out, and his arms encircled her.

But instead of the kiss she was longing for, he whispered, "Brooke, darling, there's something I must tell you."

She opened her eyes and touched her fingers lightly to his lips. "Oh, no, darling! You don't have to say anything. Just hold me."

"I'd like to hold you for as long as I live," Greg replied quietly. "But I've got something I must tell you, Brooke; something about why I'm like Jonah . . . Jonah . . . Jonah. . . ."

The thunder of the Hawaiian waterfall diminished, and the orchid in her hair vanished. Brooke was instantly awake, her heart pounding. She blinked and held her eyes open, straining to hear what had penetrated her sleep.

There was a faint slice of moon, and the myriad stars gave a little light on the desert. Brooke could see movement there, so she strained to see better.

She'd never seen a coyote outside of a zoo, but she knew instantly that's what she was seeing. But there wasn't just one; there were perhaps a dozen of them. They were scruffy, terribly skinny and untidy. There was nothing graceful about their gaunt bodies, yet they were playing like children. They circled in a carefree manner perhaps twenty feet from the Jeep.

They made a strange sound. It wasn't the familiar yapping or cry she'd heard in movies—nor the lonesome, howling call. Instead it was the most compelling sound Brooke had ever known.

She listened, enthralled. The coyotes didn't make any sound Brooke could describe, yet she understood clearly they were calling her. Instinctively, Brooke wanted to answer. She found herself irresistibly drawn to the coyotes. She wanted to play with them.

She reached for the Jeep's door and pushed the curtains back so she could get out.

"Brooke, no!" The words were hissed and low, sharp with authority, and so strong that Brooke's hand was arrested on the door handle. She glanced through the windshield at Greg's dark form. He had shifted to one elbow, facing the coyotes, but she saw the moon reflected in his eyes. They were turned toward her, inside the Jeep's blackness.

"No, Brooke!" Greg's voice was louder, more firm.

Suddenly, the coyotes broke their circle of play. They didn't repeat the sound, which had so charmed Brooke. They simply vanished like shadows into the deeper shadows of the desert night.

Greg slid unsteadily off the Jeep's hood and came around to Brooke's side. He opened the door and asked, "You all right?"

"I . . . I think so. Oh, Greg! They were calling to me! It was the most alluring sound." She was trembling and instinctively reached both hands about his neck.

"I heard them," he said, putting his arms around her. "It was a siren call like nothing I've ever heard before. Yet some years ago, I remember—"

She interrupted. "It's not the thirst?"

He shook his head. "I knew an American missionary to Baja who once had a similar experience. He wanted to answer that call, but resisted."

"Oh, Greg! What would have happened if—"

"I don't know."

"Am I losing my mind? How can a wild call sound so logical that I wanted to join those animals?"

"It doesn't matter," he said, comforting her. "It's over."

"Oh, Greg! Hold me tight!"

He drew her close but staggered slightly on his feet. She looked with alarm at his face but saw only the dark outline against the night.

"You OK?" she asked.

"A little shaky," he admitted, "but I'm not sure if it's the electrolytes or the nearness of you." His voice was low and husky as he added, "Oh, Brooke! I've waited all my life for this moment!"

Brooke stood silently in his arms, her mind swirling. Was it the maddening lack of water, which made her thoughts and emotions soar? Or was it because now she could see clearly what she had not been able to do before? Greg was the missing part of her life; the necessary link that made her life complete.

Chapter Sixteen

Before the chill of the early morning had been wiped away by the desert sun, Greg and Brooke walked the entire distance of the proposed landing strip. They turned at its far end and looked back toward the Jeep.

"What do you think, Greg?"

"I'm no pilot, but I believe somebody like Scotty could make it."

"If they find us."

"They'll find us."

He said it with such conviction Brooke glanced sharply at him. His dark beard was now a bristly mass of black, mixed with the perspiration and grit, which was so much a part of the Baja desert.

"How can you sound so confident, Greg?"

"Because, unless my electrolytes are so out of kilter that my mind is no longer functioning properly, this is the third day."

She frowned. "I'm not sure I understand."

"The third day, as I recall, was when Jonah was released by the great fish and found himself safely back on shore."

Brooke suppressed a sudden shudder of fear. She thought Greg Cameron was beginning to talk irrationally. She studied him at some length as they slowly walked back toward the Jeep. Greg's lips were chapped and cracked, and she noticed he was moving slowly, as if he were weak. Brooke was surprised to see the same was true of herself. She lifted rough, sore fingers to her own lips. But they were not nearly as dry and broken as his.

That's when she spoke up. "Greg, there was enough water left after the spill for each of us to have several swallows. But you haven't taken any, have you?"

He managed a grin, which caused a bright fleck of blood to appear on his cracked lower lip. "Ouch!" he said, gently touching the lip and looking at the spot of blood on his fingertip.

"Answer me, Greg. Please?"

He looked down at her, his eyes soft. "I don't know what you're talking about, Brooke."

"Oh, yes you do! You only pretended to take a few swallows of that remaining water."

He shook his head. "What difference does it make?"

"At least an extra half day or so before you become comatose."

He walked in silence a moment, his dark eyes glazing so visibly that Brooke was alarmed. Finally he replied, "I took just enough to wet my lips."

Brooke wondered how much closer he was to unconsciousness than she. The thought of being alone in the desert without Greg rose up inside her as a hard, dull pain.

She stepped in front of him and looked up into his eyes. "Greg, I can't tell you how much I appreciate what you were trying to do. But I don't want to be alone out here in this desert."

"Scotty'll be along," he said, lifting his eyes to search the sky.

"I hope so," Brooke said, "but I'd rather you stuck around to be with me."

He smiled, wincing as his lips cracked again. "Believe me, Brooke, I have every intention of hanging on as long as I can."

"Then let's get back in the Jeep where there is some protection from the sun. This is going to be a scorcher of a day!"

At the vehicle, Greg removed the rearview mirror and dusted it with the piece of sack he had used for a pillow. "In case they fly by today, I can reflect the sun into the cockpit with this thing," he explained.

"Think it'll work?"

"Beats shouting," he said with a grin.

Brooke watched the sunlight bounce off the glass and into the brassy sky as Greg practiced with the mirror. It might be a futile gesture, she thought, but it was certainly worth trying.

Her thirst had slowly built until she had a near-maddening passion for anything cold and wet. Her tongue was so thick and dry it seemed to clack in her mouth, and she found it increasingly difficult to talk. By noon, the Jeep was an oven, even with the curtains up and the windshield opened. They seemed to be baking alive, even in the shade.

"Greg, I think I'd better say this before talking becomes too difficult."

"What's that, Brooke?" he said as he turned in the driver's seat to look her in the eye.

"I'm sorry I set you up during that television interview, and I feel bad about some of the verbal fights we've had. Forgive me for being so stupid."

"I've been just as much at fault, probably more so," he admitted, trying to lick his dry lips. "I guess I've been trying too hard to avoid a couple of things that were inevitable."

"Such as?"

"Trying to keep from falling in love with you, for one."

He said it so casually, she looked up at him in surprise. She wasn't quite sure he'd really said the words until he continued.

"But I couldn't stop myself. So I did the next best thing by trying to keep you from seeing me as anything but an undesirable suitor."

She frowned. "Why would you do that?"

"So you'd not fall in love with me, and I'd not have to tell you how unsure I am. I'm almost like two persons.

"One is the doctor that most people know about. He has a playboy image and only associates with San Francisco's executive establishment."

"And the other person, Greg?"

"A part of me I've never let you see clearly."

"You mean the doctor who loves kids and will do everything he can to help them?"

"Something like that; yes."

She was silent a moment, thinking. Then she

said, "Want to tell me about the other person?"

"Yes, but first I'd like you to tell me something. . . . I'd like to know what you were doing awake so long last night."

"How'd you know that?"

"Because I was awake, too, staring up at the stars and thinking. Well, to be honest, I was praying."

"Strange as it seems, that's what I was doing, too," she admitted.

He looked at her and smiled. "Anything you'd care to tell me?"

Brooke paused, not really sure she wanted to tell Greg what she had promised the Lord. But she knew if she didn't, it would be breaking her commitment.

"I was a Christian through most of upper elementary, junior high, and high school. But at a missionary conference when I was sixteen, I decided I had made a big mistake."

"How so?" Greg inquired.

"Oh, it was a combination of a lot of things, but let me take a stab at it. Daddy had just bought me a car, and most of my friends at school had money to do almost anything they wanted. Looking classy was a mark of status, so I made an effort to make sure I had a closet full of stylish clothes. I knew that none of those missionaries had the money to go on a shopping spree at Saks Fifth Avenue, and I began to notice that almost no one was wearing what New York and Paris said was in style for that season. Now that I look back on the incident, I realize everyone looked just fine. But in my sixteen-year-old mind, I concluded that my friends would only laugh at everyone's lack of taste for fashion.

She hesitated, so Greg looked uncertainly into her eyes. Then he asked, "So you took back your commitment because you thought God might someday want you to join them and become a missionary?"

"Something like that. Anyway, I determined that I was old enough to decide whether or not I wanted to go to youth group and Sunday school, so I quit. When I got into college, many of my professors said God couldn't possibly exist. And I started believing them."

He let her words hang in the still, hot air for a moment before asking softly, "And last night?"

She looked him squarely in the eyes. "I prayed, Greg, because I realized that only God could have created stars—and even the animals and the desert and you and I. Since he created us, he would care about what was happening—and understand my fear."

"Weren't you afraid when Scotty's plane lost power over that canyon?"

"Yes, and that's when I first realized I still believed in God. But last night, well, I made a recommitment of my life to him."

"Will you feel that way tomorrow when we're safely home?"

She smiled, feeling the pain of her chapped, cracked lips. "I thought of that. Yes, whether we live through this or they find our bodies here in this desert, I'll feel the same way. In the blackness of these Baja nights, I've realized what's really important."

"And what's that, Brooke?"

"Just being alive, to begin with. Then finding and marrying the right man, having a family, and doing it all as Christ taught us to."

"And have you found that man, Brooke?"

For a moment, she didn't know how to answer. Then she forced a smile. "I'm not sure. Maybe I have. . . ." She looked into his eyes, remembering the touch of his lips on hers. But the moment soon was lost. . . .

"Listen!" he said, taking a deep breath, and then stiffening.

Brooke heard it, too. "A plane!" She leaped from the Jeep so suddenly she tore her sleeve on the open door's handle, but she didn't care. She ran into the open, sweeping the sky with her hands and waving the instant she saw the glint of silver wings in the distance.

"Here! Over here!"

She knew it was a futile gesture, but she jumped up and down, surprised at how weak she was and how light-headed she felt.

Greg was standing well away from the Jeep, his legs braced, the mirror tilted toward the sun. Brooke saw his wrists moving rapidly, and the sun reflected back into the sky toward the plane. But she couldn't be sure it was coming anywhere near the tiny spot of silver, which marked the plane's distant course.

"Oh, Lord," she moaned, "let them see us!"

The plane flew on, far out in the distance, a gnat-sized symbol of hope and life. Greg's mirror worked furiously, Brooke saw, and he was perspiring with the intensity of his efforts and the boiling sun.

The sound died away. Slowly, the desert grew silent again, except for Brooke's quiet sobs. She sank wearily to the sand, her thirst returning with a vengeance. Death seemed much closer for both her and Greg.

Chapter Seventeen

Brooke did not cry. She simply sat on the sand, feeling strangely light-headed. Yet, somehow, she felt a peace she couldn't explain. When Scotty's plane had flown on without any indication of spotting them, she had resigned herself to death. Surprisingly, she could accept that knowledge, even though everything in her wanted to live.

Greg's shadow fell over her, and she felt a momentary sense of relief as the brass sun was shielded from her body. She felt his arms raise her. The power in him transmitted itself to her, and she forced her knees to lock and she stood upright; her head tipped up to face him.

"That was it, wasn't it, Greg? Our last chance?"

"Not necessarily." He spoke with difficulty, his horribly chapped and broken lips moving slowly. He stood so his head shaded her face and she could see how emotionally drained he was. He continued, "I'm not sure if this is the third day or not. My head's mixed up and I've lost track of time."

"No matter," Brooke said, trying to reflect the peace she felt within. "I'm prepared to accept whatever comes. But if I could fight something solid or tangible, I'd attack with everything in me—just to stay alive."

He led her slowly back to the hot shadows of the Jeep and helped her settle into the passenger's seat. Then he walked around the hood and crawled under the steering wheel before he said anything.

"Brooke," he began at last, "I don't want to die, either. And yet I know, medically speaking, I'm not many hours from unconsciousness."

"I know," she said softly, laying a hand gritty with the desert's fine, invisible sand on the back of his. "We're both closer than I'd like, but at least I've made my peace with God." She hesitated, then asked, "What about you, Greg?"

He moved his fingers slowly so his hand covered hers. "To answer that, my darling, I must first tell you what I promised before that plane flew by."

Her head snapped sharply around. Had he said, "my darling?" or had her mind played tricks?

"I regret, far more than I can tell you, having you involved in this situation. I've asked God to spare your life; in fact, that's why I faked drinking the water."

He didn't blame her for the loss of the life saving water, and she was sure the way he went right on with his thoughts that it wasn't a diplomatic gesture.

"My career was the most important thing in the world to me, too, Brooke. For a man, that's not too unusual, I guess. But there's one part of my life and career that nobody knows about. Well," he said, shifting his fingers around hers and looking fully at her, "perhaps you got an inkling when that picture fell out of my wallet."

Brooke blinked, trying to understand. Strange how prolonged lack of water could make your head so funny you couldn't grasp simple things. "I'm sorry," she said, feeling her thick, dry tongue clack in her mouth, "but I don't understand."

"My brain's not functioning right, Brooke, and my thoughts are wandering. I probably sound terribly thick-tongued, too. But I've got to say it, even if it doesn't make sense to you yet. Maybe you've seen some stories about me in the newspaper? I'm always written up with the lie I told them way back in the beginning.

"But I'm not the son of a wealthy Argentine rancher and his former beauty-queen wife. I've never been there. I was reared in a good Christian home, but I hated what my parents did, so I tried to deny my heritage."

He paused, swallowing hard and trying to speak clearly when his mental processes were being wrecked by the imbalance of electrolytes. Brooke said nothing, so he continued.

"I speak Spanish because that was my first language. My father was an American missionary to the State of Tabasco. That's along the south coast of the Gulf of Mexico. His first wife died shortly after dad arrived there to serve the people. Dad remarried. She was one of the local women whom he had led to Christ. She was my mother."

Brooke thought she heard his voice break, but she wasn't sure if it was from emotion or from the mental strain of talking when thirst was so dominant.

Greg turned and looked out across the desert. He didn't look at Brooke as he continued. "When I was about ten, I felt God's call on my life. I felt I should go to the United States and become a medical missionary to my mother's people. So I prepared, and finally went to study in American universities and medical schools. But somewhere along the line I lost my faith. I became ashamed of my father's calling and my mother's people."

He turned back to her but released her hand and gripped the steering wheel with both hands, leaning forward against the wheel. "I made up a family history, gave my father wealth and my mother beauty—which she really did have—and created a whole new image for myself as a society doctor. But my conscience sometimes bothered me, so I'd quietly do things nobody knew."

Brooke guessed, "Like operating on the little pig girl?"

He nodded, still looking through the windshield. "But sometimes I'd miss my faith, so I'd slip into some little out-of-the-way church, like the one where we saw each other. . . . I was still feeling God's call on my life but—like Jonah—I kept running away."

"Oh, Greg!" Brooke's fingers moved compassionately to touch his arm. "Oh, Greg!" She didn't know what else to say.

He turned and took her hand, holding it against his arm where she'd placed it. "Brooke, I thought maybe God would spare me, as he did Jonah, and this desert would spew us out on the third day, because I recommitted my life to him. But last night, lying awake there on the hood, I was afraid it was too late for me. I still hope you'll be rescued, but—"

He didn't finish, and Brooke understood why. She said huskily, feeling the dryness of her mouth, "It's all right, Greg."

He shook his head. "No, it's not. I've not only lost my own life, but I've cost yours, too. For that, I'm truly sorry. Can you forgive me?"

She leaned against his shoulder. "There's nothing to forgive. I had run away from God, too. It seems like a harsh penalty for us to pay, but I have peace."

Suddenly, he stiffened, and she tensed, knowing instinctively he had heard something. He grabbed the mirror and was out of the Jeep, staggering to regain his balance.

Brooke slid out onto the sand. She cupped her hands over her eyes and looked toward the sound.

"There!" she cried, pointing. "Three of them! All three planes!"

They were flying a search pattern, Brooke realized, spread out and flying low, but within sight of each other. She recognized the high single-winged Cessna the nurse had piloted down, and the low-winged planes Scotty and the dentist flew.

"Oh, Greg!" she cried, running to him. "Make them see us! Make them see us!"

He was working the mirror furiously, reflecting the sun toward the cockpit of the nearest plane, the Cessna.

But the planes droned on and again the silence settled down. The desert wind rose, filling the sky with a low, moaning sound that reflected the anguish of the man and woman who stood wearily in the desolation.

Darkness came again, but neither man nor woman spoke. They did not eat. Everything was concentrated in the body's screaming demand for what it could not have: water.

The night was even more awesome than before. Nothing Brooke had ever seen compared to the Baja blackness of the Vizcaino Desert. She longed for something to break the ground's darkness: a kerosene lamp in a remote home, a campfire, or even the glowing end of a worker's cigarette. But there was nothing except the silent, almost solid blackness.

Greg was a long time getting up onto the hood. Brooke was fearful he'd not awake in the morning; she wasn't even sure she'd be alive at dawn, either. She seemed in a sort of stupor, sitting uncomfortably in the right front seat, her long legs draped across the driver's seat. She wasn't sure as she began to slip into soft, silent sleep if this was the beginning of a comatose condition, or merely sleep.

Brooke floated in and out of this dazelike sleep. Once as she turned uncomfortably in the narrow seat, she heard a noise above her.

She stared out the windshield at Greg's quiet form. He still lay on his back, his long legs hanging down over the headlights. The Baja night was still the blackest she had ever seen, but there was enough light from the stars that she could clearly see the ground around them.

Brooke moved her head and felt it touch the underside of the canvas roof. Her eyes went up and noticed that the roof sagged heavily. Slowly, uncertainly, she reached her open palm up and pushed gently on the bulge. It seemed to shift slightly so Brooke shoved harder.

Instantly, the sagging section moved, and there was a protesting sound. Brooke jerked her hand back as a large bobcat leaped from the canvas roof to land beside Greg's sleeping figure on the hood. Greg sat up, startled, as the cat bounded lightly to the ground.

Brooke and Greg watched the bobcat as it walked slowly across the open ground, with its short, stubby tail twitching behind.

Greg turned slowly to look into the windshield. "You OK?" he asked quietly.

Still shaking, Brooke nodded. "Just scared," she admitted with a raspy laugh.

"We were both so quiet that he decided to rest in the softest spot around."

"But—he must have walked right by you to get up on that roof!"

"Maybe so, I'm not too alert just now. You going to be all right?"

"I . . . I don't know."

"Would you feel safer if I came inside for a while?" he said hoarsely, his voice faltering with each word.

Brooke hesitated, then nodded her head in agreement. She watched as he slowly lowered himself off the hood and walked weakly around to the driver's side of the Jeep.

"I love you," he whispered as he carefully slid

into the seat beside her.

"And I love you, Greg," she said, very softly and with total assurance.

They kissed automatically, but each flinched and drew back from the pain of cracked, blistered, and swollen lips.

"Not very romantic, my darling," Greg whispered.

"Oh, yes it is, Greg! Kissing can wait, but hold me close! Hold me forever, no matter what happens!"

She nestled against his shoulder and rested there, content to be with him, even if death was closing in fast.

There was a hotness against Brooke's cheek. And some throbbing sound was bothering her. Without opening her eyes, she brushed at the warmth. It didn't go away. She tried again, but there was no change. With an effort, she forced her eyelids up.

Immediately, she closed them. The morning sun was burning through the windshield and striking her face. She moved her head backward into the shade of the covered Jeep. She opened her eyes again. They stayed open.

Then she saw Greg.

He was leaning against the steering wheel, his unshaven, black whiskers bristling darkly in the sun. But his eyes were open, and in his hand, being waved weakly back and forth, was the mirror.

"I thought I was dreaming," he said with thick-tongued difficulty, "but I finally came to, and there they were." The mirror kept moving, slowly, but with great determination.

Brooke's eyes saw through the heavy dust on the windshield. Three planes were approaching!

"Didn't want to wake you in case I couldn't make them see me," Greg explained weakly. "But they're flying straight at us. Every one of those pilots should be blinded by now, the way I've been hitting their cockpits with light."

"Oh, Lord!" Brooke wasn't even aware she'd said it. "Oh, Lord God! Make them see us! Make them—"

"Hey!" Greg's voice wasn't loud, but it was full of joy. "Look! They're wagging their wings! What a sight! What a sight!"

The three planes converged within a few hundred feet of each other and flew over so low the Jeep's canvas top was almost torn loose by the blast. Then the planes pulled apart, circled, and fell in behind each other. Scotty's single-engined aircraft took the lead, leveling out and settling down on the far end of the hard-packed, nearly level desert sand.

"Thank you, Lord!" Greg said, his hand dropping the mirror.

"Amen," Brooke whispered. Then she turned her face to Greg. Tiredly, but with the strength of new life and hope, he slid his arm about her and pulled her close. They kissed, and this time, neither was aware of pain.